IN A CORNER,

Darkly

MORE REASONS TO KEEP THE LIGHTS ON

SUE ROVENS

ISBN: 1491258896
ISBN 13: 9781491258897

For my dad, Seymour Rovens, who loved to read.
(1924 – 1984)

IN A CORNER, Darkly

Volume 2

PREFACE

When I was in high school, I was obsessed with a rock band. I had collected every album, every picture, and every article from papers and magazines that I could find. This was years before the internet, so locating this information took serious research and time. I wrote letters and sent birthday cards to the members, saw a number of concerts, and generally spent every free moment trying to figure out how to find one more snippet of gossip or photo I didn't already own. After three years of this obsessive teen-age behavior, my dad said to me, "If you put as much energy into anything else like you do for this music group, you'll be able to do anything."

It's been over thirty-five years since he said that.

In 2009, after telling some people that I was going to write a book, I didn't hear much in the way of support. There had been quite a number of naysayers, quick to point out that many people *say* they are going to write a book, but very few actually do.

In 2012, In a Corner, Darkly: Volume 1 was published. My dad wasn't alive to see it, but I believe he knows.

I'm not certain if he would have liked the stories in *this* book. He was more into history, having had an amazing memory for dates and details. But I personally don't recall if he was too interested in horror and suspense.

He did, however, take me to see *The Shining* when it first came out. I slept with the lights on for an entire week.

TABLE OF CONTENTS

FUNERAL GAMES

Who doesn't love an eye-catching book with an irresistible blurb on the back? My preferred genre is horror. I *love* a good horror story. There's nothing I would rather do than relax on my couch during a rainy Sunday afternoon with a pot of Oolong tea and a great Stephen King or Jack Ketchum tome.

But, if after a few pages, I realize that the book I purchased is actually a story about aliens instead of good old fashioned creepy suspense, I end up feeling duped, like somebody got away with bloody murder and took my money – all because of false advertising. It's not a personal affront to writers of sci-fi or fantasy, nor is it a criticism of stories that have to do with interplanetary tropes. I simply never liked it when a title suggested *one* genre but the chapters inside belonged to *another*.

Recently, I was wandering through the aisles of a local bookstore in search of something new and exciting to read. A glossy covered volume, complete with a decrepit headstone tilted to its side managed to catch my eye. Its title was <u>Funeral Games</u>. Unfortunately, by the time I found it, I was in a bit of a hurry and didn't have an opportunity to thumb through it first. I bought it strictly by the cover and title alone.

I was meeting my friend Gayle for lunch at a place we jokingly referred to as *Che Hair.* Years ago, we had the displeasure of finding a small, thin, blonde hair resting atop a cucumber and tomato appetizer. Although we were pretty disgusted, we kept returning for our monthly lunch dates. It was cheap, close to where we lived, and the only vegetarian restaurant in town. We made a conscious decision to give them the benefit of the doubt. But if we were feeling particularly snarky on a given afternoon, we would tell them to 'hold the hair' after placing our order.

After my lunch with Gayle, sans extra hair, I headed home with the sole intent of delving into this new yarn for the rest of the afternoon. Both Bella and Noodle, my cats, joined me on the couch, each taking turns rubbing their cheeks against the pointed corners of the new book.

"You know, neither of you are starved for attention, you silly kitties," I told them as I petted their heads. After what they must have deemed to be *enough*, they settled themselves near my feet and promptly dozed off.

I flipped past the forward and the introduction and started to read chapter one. After the first few sentences, my initial excitement had plummeted and I felt like I had been had.

"...when I came home from my cousin Vince's funeral, I sensed something familiar. Something felt like I had lived through this before; like I had traveled through time."

Shit.

I had always considered the subject of time travel to be part of science fiction, maybe even fantasy, but certainly not horror. The further I read into chapter one, the more the author talked of black holes and time rifts. I was literally seconds from closing the book for good. Instead, I turned the page. The title of chapter two compelled me. I was hooked. I read the rest of the book in one sitting; bathroom and snack breaks be damned.

Chapter Two: How the Dead Follow You Home After a Funeral.

I devoured the next twelve chapters and didn't let up until I hit the bibliography on page 184. I placed the book on the coffee table in front of the couch. What I had learned over the past few hours didn't sit well with me. I felt a chill through my body even though my hands were damp with sweat. I was trembling. The motion woke both cats from their sleep and they were not amused.

I didn't like what I read. In fact, I hated it.

According to <u>Funeral Games</u>, if certain entities are aligned perfectly such as the time of day, the position of the planets, oceanic tides, and an unsuspecting host, the dead have an *open window*. In other words, they can follow someone home and take up residence with them. They become opportunists and the longer the dead remain with the living, the more prominent their physical appearance might become.

The example given in the book was as follows: *an unusual sensation will become a ghostly apparition. After more time passes, that ghostly apparition might start to take on an actual physical presence, like a skeleton. It might evolve from there or not. The manifestation is different in every circumstance.*

According to chapter five, reports of witnessing a bundle of nerves hovering in backyards -- *just the nervous system and nothing else,* were driving people to madness. Others explained how internal organs like lungs or a liver had shown up in their bed or bathtub. Apparently, they tried to dispose of these ghoulish anatomical parts, even going so far as to call the police. Yet regardless of what they did, the pieces returned.

I concluded that the whole thing sounded like a bunch of rubbish. It was a waste of fifteen dollars and a perfectly good afternoon and evening. I should have stopped at chapter one, if not sooner and I was mentally kicking myself for turning that blasted page to chapter two. But something about it crept under my skin. Why couldn't I have simply skipped over the more haunting parts? It's not like my mind would replay some of the more ghastly stories when I'm alone with the lights off and the doors locked.

Would it?

Ever since moving into my own home a few years ago, I rationalized away any strange noise I heard by playing the *logic game.* The grinding sound from the kitchen was only the ice maker from the refrigerator; not a deranged lunatic testing out his chainsaw. A dull, repetitive thump, thump, thump from the basement meant that the dryer was on its second cycle; not an angry psychopath tossing decapitated heads down the staircase. And any thunderous scuffles from another room were only the cats playing. It was absolutely not a cannibalistic lunatic in search of a human meal. But having just finished a book in which the dead could choose someone to cohabitate with, the *logic game* became impossible to win.

Two weeks prior to reading the book, I had attended my uncle's funeral. He was eighty-nine and had been sick for quite a while. His passing didn't come as a surprise to anyone in the family, but it was still sad and there were tears of mourning. Because of that recent experience, I couldn't shake the disturbing passage from chapter four:

They come between midnight and three. No lock or barrier can stop them since they are part of the spirit world. The dead are partial to setting up their new residence with relatives.

Still, I couldn't use the book as an excuse. I had to get to sleep. My co-workers would not be very sympathetic if I stayed up too late worrying and ended up oversleeping. I turned the volume up on the alarm. By sheer will and determination, I forced myself to sleep.

It was close to three in the morning when I woke up from hearing an unusual noise downstairs. I rubbed my eyes, still half asleep, as I navigated the steps. Assuming the cats had decided to have a nightly game of WWF (World Wrestling Felines), I called out for them, but neither came. I yelled louder, but there was still no response.

I rounded the corner to the kitchen, ready to flip the light switch on, when I saw a glimpse of a hideous being. I sucked my breath back into my throat. *Was I still dreaming?* No, I must have seen it wrong. I peered around the wall again.

There, in the far corner of my kitchen stood a skeleton. Not a plastic classroom replica or one from a science study kit, but a six foot actual nightmare. The pallor of its bones practically shimmered in the moonlight which was streaming in through the partially open blinds. The cadaver wore no clothes but sported a few random swathes of decaying skin and bits of connective tissue. It must have knocked a glass off of the counter because a blue tumbler was rolling back and forth on the old linoleum floor. That must have been the sound I heard.

I stood watching, terrified and frozen with disgust and fear. My brain couldn't grasp the reality of the situation. *I had to be dreaming* - that's the only explanation that made sense. Skeletons don't walk around by themselves -- *they can't!* It's anatomically impossible. There are no muscles to move body parts, no brain to send signals, no nerves to activate anything. I had taken physiology in college. I had a basic grasp of how a human body functions. What I was witnessing was against all reason.

The corpse tapped its finger bones on the counter, as if it was growing impatient. The clacking sound reverberated through my *own* body. It walked with a staccato gait next to the counter until it reached the cat food container. As it proceeded to pry the lid off, the food pellets rattled against the sides. The familiar noise coaxed my pets out of hiding. The prospect of being fed apparently was stronger than their sense of fear and uncertainty. I watched the skeleton pour kibble onto the floor as both cats seized the opportunity to eat. The corpse put the container back on the counter, bent down, and ran a bony finger along Bella's fur. It was then that the skull turned and looked directly at me.

I couldn't speak, let alone move - not that it would have mattered. Could this ghastly thing hear me? Or see me?

A passage from the book flashed into my head. The author explained that the dead who followed people home from the grave were not necessarily dangerous. Their only desire was to be among the living again, no matter what form they took. If that meant this walking cadaver would make an appearance every night in my home, what could I do?

I reached for the phone and dialed 9-1-1. When the operator asked what the emergency was, I hung up. *What the hell was I going to say?* An animated corpse just fed my cats, could you please send a squad car?

It rose to its feet and erratically shuffled toward me. I backed up and screamed. I clasped my hands together and held them against my gut. I couldn't bear the thought of that hideous thing touching me - my soft, pliable, pink living flesh making contact with its own calcified skeletal bones. It raised a pointed finger to its perpetual grin as if to shush me. I felt nauseated and dizzy.

As it moved closer, I backed up against the living room wall. For the briefest of moments, I entertained the idea of running upstairs to the bedroom and locking the door. If I were *really quick*, I might be able to sidestep it and take off down the street. But to be honest, even if the neighbors came to my rescue, I couldn't live with the image of seeing a corpse spasmodically chase after me. That alone would cause me to go mad.

I shut my eyes, sank down into a ball on the floor, and waited for this night terror to end. I prayed that I would wake up and find myself in bed with both cats, safe and alone, with only a fading memory of a frightful dream.

When I opened my eyes, it was the following morning. I was lying in bed with the blankets pulled up around my shoulders. Both Bella and Noodle were sleeping on my left side, curled up with their tails over their faces, quietly purring. I thought about the previous night, but with the bright sun streaming in through the white curtains, everything from the day before simply faded away. Reading <u>Funeral Games</u> must have kicked my vivid imagination into overdrive. I promised myself to give the darn book to whoever was hosting the first garage sale of the year.

When I arrived at work, I mentioned my dream and the foul book that started it all to a few select co-workers. No one had read it, but one person admitted to hearing similar stories on a talk show a few months back. It seemed that everyone I talked to had some kind of story to share about imaginations running wild; how their minds played frightening tricks on them, usually in the middle of the night.

Once I was home for the day, I threw a Lean Cuisine into the microwave, punched a few buttons, and sat down on the couch. As I reached for the TV remote, the cover of the book caught my eye. I picked it up. A yellow sticky note protruded from the center.

I didn't put any note in that book.

I opened it up to the flagged section.

Chapter 6: When the Dead Come Calling

"...when the bodies returned every night, sometimes they brought others. I couldn't believe the repulsive abomination before me. They danced. These horrid creatures actually danced in my basement. There was no music but some of the disembodied hands clapped in rhythm as the headless torsos and legs spun around.

My husband tried to chase them away on many occasions, sometimes even grabbing these atrocities and physically throwing them out our door. But I swear on a stack of Bibles, they came back. Every night at 12:01am, we could hear those hellacious beings downstairs, cavorting with each other, going through our closets, rummaging around our laundry room, pretending to be alive again."

- Harriet, West Virginia

I didn't feel like eating anymore.

Outside, the evening began to pull its shades on the sky. Mindlessly, I watched television until I couldn't keep my eyes open anymore. I picked Bella up and hugged her. Noodle followed at my heels. I spoke to them as I settled into bed and turned off the lights. I felt as each cat found their own space on top of the blankets and curl up. Listening to their purrs calmed my nerves and I drifted off to sleep.

I woke up to the familiar buzz of my alarm early the next morning. I went through my normal routine of showering, dressing, and brushing my hair. I headed downstairs, calling out for Bella and Noodle, expecting them to come running for breakfast, but neither came.

I turned the corner to the kitchen, looked down, and saw kibble scattered across the linoleum floor. On the counter lay a distal phalanx - the first segment of a finger bone.

FOR THE GOOD OF SOCIETY

For the record, I am completely against having ice picks shoved into my eyes in order to scramble my brain. That's what they want to do though. Scramble it so I'll be complacent, just like everyone else. Just like my damn buddies. Just like my poor sap neighbors. But I'd do anything to keep that from happening to me. *And* to my parents. The main thing I need to do is not let them find me. I have to believe and trust in myself or I'll go insane.

My proper name is Garrison Holmes, but I usually go by Gully. I'm sixteen and live with my mom and dad. And even though I work full-time and don't really have friends anymore, I still have dreams.

Color. I dream that the world is full of color. In my reality, everything here is grey or brown or some sickening shade of puke. Our clothes are shapeless patches made of scratchy burlap, our houses sit in rows, jutting up against one another so there's barely a strip of dead grass on which to trample or walk a mangy dog. Every meal is pretty much the same. The only difference is what shade of boring is being served that day. It's not my mom's fault. She does the best she can with the few choices we're given every month in our box of supplies.

Most of the older adults don't talk about it much, but you know how rumors spread. After some wacked out election went haywire about twenty years ago, our country went from being *number one in the world* to persona non grata; no one wanted anything to do with us. We weren't allowed to travel to other countries anymore. All imports and exports stopped. Every school closed from lack of money and support. Worst of all, technology came to a complete halt. People stopped caring, stopped helping each other, and only started looking out for themselves.

My family had always been close; my parents and I. They made sure that I always had what I needed -- food, clothes, blankets, soap. When I was a little kid, they would tell me stories about how things were *before*...

I think that's when my dreams began. They painted such luscious images. Bountiful pictures swirled through my head; plump juicy oranges, fire-engine red strawberries dotted with perfectly lined seeds embedded in their skins, and ice-chilled watermelon cut into crisp triangular wedges with black seeds burrowed into the inner rosy flesh like a spotted Dalmatian puppy. I could listen to their stories all night long. Oftentimes, I tried to stay awake, begging them to keep talking, but sleep always managed to lull me into its grip, dark and alone.

That's how everybody seems to live now – alone. Maybe stand-offish is a better word. With no outside help from other countries, we had to become completely independent. It sounds pretty good, doesn't it? Being independent? Maybe in some circumstances it is, but not when lunatics are running the show. Food prices were normal at first, but after a while the farmers didn't want to grow anything for anyone else. Same thing happened with construction and tailors and doctors and teachers. It was like everybody in the country went on one big strike.

That's when the government took over. They began by assigning jobs and organizing all day-to-day operations. Wages were pathetic regardless of what job you held. I think the doctors made the most, if you could say $12,000 a year was something to brag about. My parents, who worked as harvesters (formerly known as farmers), brought home about $2,500 a year. Sanitation workers like me enjoyed $1,100 for the fruits of our labor – hardly worth getting out of bed for in my book.

I *want* books. I *want* the movies that my parents told me about, even if they were dumb or silly. I *want* to watch bad television and surf the internet and hang out at the mall with friends. But ever since that election, the internet disappeared, followed by movies, books, and magazines. Apparently, there wasn't time for *frivolous things*. There was too much work to do now that we were on our own. Museums and art galleries were torn down in order to use the land for harvesting. Shopping malls and restaurants were turned into factories. Libraries were burned down out of spite. But at least we have plenty of gun ranges and bars.

There's only vocational training now -- things like nursing, cooking, plumbing, heating. A person begins their government-assigned schooling around their eighth birthday. I had no desire for sanitation duty, but that's what I was assigned to do.

I tried to like it. *I swear I tried.* I even had a few friends for a while, but I was going crazy. Not the kind of crazy *they* mean, but the kind where I couldn't stand doing the same crap day in and day out six days a week. That's everybody's schedule; six days on and one lousy day off. There's no vacation time, no sick days, no holiday. That joy ride ended when everything went to hell back in 2016.

There has to be more to life than emptying shit from outhouses and scooping up garbage from the back lots of tract homes. When you look up in the sky and see clouds of regurgitated smoke belching out from factory warehouses, you feel nothing but despondent. When questions are discouraged and the mere concept of thinking outside the box is regarded as treason, the will to live dissolves like an ice cube dropped head first into a cup of boiling water.

About a week ago while I was at work, a great idea came to me. I played out the scenario in my head a few times so I wouldn't forget anything. I knew better than to commit it to paper. In a world where every shred of information has the potential for being scrutinized, the greatest ideas are best left unwritten.

My plan was to leave the country, to head up north to Canada. While everyone was on break at work, I would take my rig and drive straight up Route 25 as far as I could go and then turn off onto Highway 3 until I crossed the border. I could drive the hell out of my truck if I had to. I was the best driver in my class for two years running. I could pull a hairpin in six seconds flat. I was confident and the more I thought about it, the more excited I got.

But that was a problem.

Being excited about something. Standing out from the ordinary. Getting emotional. That kind of behavior leads to the ice picks coming out to play.

I chose Canada because it was close. I wouldn't have minded Europe or Asia. Hell, even parts of Africa would have been acceptable. Any place where people had access to the internet, and books, and movies. A country where they didn't assign you to a particular job. A place where you could think for yourself and not be forced to conform in every way imaginable.

Early in my life, I learned that the biggest mistake people would make when trying to escape was blabbing about it. They'd get nervous and tell somebody and before you knew it, the police would drag 'em away in irons. It wasn't bad – *it was inconceivable.* It was as if the very gates of hell opened their fiery doors, threw out a burning welcome mat, and shoved a party horn in the guy's mouth. By the time they got done with him, the poor sap would be a shell of who he was.

Once you see someone go through *reconstitution*, you never forget it. The image gets seared into your brain and for the rest of your life, that mental picture keeps you on the straight and narrow. It had for *me*. We aren't scared of things like ghosts or vampires or witches. Stuff like that is dumb. Stuff like that is childish. There's a *real* boogeyman, and he happens to carry ice picks.

If you get caught trying to leave the country or act rebellious in any way, the government will send their security after you, toss you down on a gurney, strap you in, and affix your head so it won't move around. Then the Boogeyman enters the scene with his two ice picks. You know the kind. You might even have a few in a kitchen drawer at home.

With the flair of a surgeon crossed with a magician, the good doctor will proceed to ram these metal instruments into your eye sockets, right between your eyeballs and your eyebrows. For the next two or three minutes, he'll swish the picks back and forth, scrambling the front part of your brain like a pile of tasteless eggs. Once they finish with you, a nurse will sew up the holes and release you from the table. Did I mention that you would be awake the whole time? This whole nightmare happens while the person is conscious. No gas, no shots, no warning, and certainly no consent.

The result of this procedure leaves you totally complacent; no more questioning authority and no more plans to leave the country. You're left with the mind of a malleable child, poised to take orders. Personally, I'd rather die first.

But now, I was ready. I wasn't going to tell anyone at work. I knew better than to make a mistake like that. The only people I could trust were my parents. I was their only child. We all took care of each other. Hell, I was hoping that they might decide to come with me. So, I talked to them that night over dinner.

Our house isn't much to look at, but then again, neither is anyone else's. We have the basics -- couch, chairs, kitchen table, beds. My mom took some of my old clothes and made curtains for the windows. My dad built a kind of make-shift greenhouse out of some slabs of lumber that he found so that my mom could try and grow a few flowers. It looked more like an outhouse without the crescent moon on the door, but at least he made the effort. Like I said, we were really close regardless of how sparse our home was.

My mom had made some spaghetti and served it with a small salad and bread. There wasn't much meat these days, but we all got our share of carbs and *then* some. It was cheap and easy and a real no-brainer for the government food supply houses.

After nervously wavering back and forth through most of the meal, I finally spoke up.

"Dad, Mom? I gotta tell you guys something."

"Sure, son. What's on your mind?"

"I'm leaving. I'm getting the hell out of here and I want you guys to come with me."

Their faces lit up like carnival barkers pegging a new, young mark. They pushed their chairs back from the table and stood up. My dad slapped me on the shoulder and shook my hand, congratulating me for being so courageous and daring.

"Gully, that's wonderful to hear," my dad said, still pumping my hand with his. "I don't think your mother and I could be more proud. Here, let me give you a little help."

He reached into his back pocket and pulled out his wallet.

"No. No, Dad. I don't want your money. I just want both of you with me."

"Please," he insisted as he folded a ten dollar bill into my sweaty palm. "Take it. For emergencies."

I looked over at my mom, but she just stood there with a big grin on her face, nodding.

"This is a special day, dear," she said. "If I'd have known you were making such an important announcement, I would have had a dessert ready."

I shook my head. "No. I don't need anything like that, Mom. All I want is for you guys to leave with me. You know, to someplace better."

"Where *are* you going, son?" Mom asked.

"Canada."

My parents looked at each other and continued to nod.

"We understand you feeling this way," Dad said. "I think I can speak for your mother when I say that Canada does have its own appeal."

They sat back down at the table and pulled their chairs in. I followed their lead.

"Do you have a date in mind?" Mom asked as she took a bite of salad. A wayward radish fell from her fork and rolled under the counter by the sink.

"This Saturday. I'm gonna leave during my second break at work."

My parents continued eating as I outlined the details of my plan.

"I really can't stress enough how much I want you guys along. We could be so much happier there, you know? I mean, aren't you sick of this shitty food and these pathetic clothes? And with nothing fun or educational to do but work for *them*?"

Their faces fell slightly and I was sorry for ruining the moment.

"Oh, oh, gosh, Mom. I'm sorry. It's-it's not your fault," I backpedaled.

"No, Gully. I understand," she said, laying a hand on my arm. "I know what you meant."

"Son," my dad started, "it's not that easy to just pick up and leave. I'm sure you know that. No son. This is all on you. I'm just glad that you had the courage to share this very grown up choice with us. Thank *you*, my boy. Thank *you*."

My body felt like a balloon meeting a sharp pin. My shoulders sank as I deflated against the back of my chair. I pushed my plate to the center of the table.

"Well," I said, "we still have three days together."

"We better make the most of them then. Don't you agree, dear?"

Mom just nodded and brushed aside a tear.

By Saturday, I became painfully aware that I might not see my parents again. Even though I had tried every conceivable argument to convince them to join me, I failed. They just reiterated that it wasn't feasible for *them* to leave, but they were happy for *my* decision to do so.

That night, about thirty minutes before I was to leave for my overnight shift, Mom and Dad stepped into the kitchen doorway with tears in their eyes.

"What?" I asked.

"We're just...a little emotional right now, Gully. You can understand that, can't you?"

I nodded. *Of course I could.* I was pretty emotional myself. I got up from the table and went over to hug them.

"You know," I said, "it's not too late. I can hide you in the rig until we cross the border." Mom and Dad opened their arms and embraced me. The three of us squished up against the doorway, crying and laughing and hugging. It must have been quite a sight.

"Does...does this mean you will? Oh, gosh, that's great! I'll help you guys pack right this second."

Dad led me back to the kitchen table with Mom in tow. He eyed the clock before we sat down. I had less than twenty minutes before I had to be at work.

"Son...Gully...Garrison...we have a surprise for you," my dad sputtered, trying not to choke up on his words.

"What? What is it?"

Mom couldn't contain herself any longer. She hopped right out of the kitchen chair, clapping her hands together as if she was a little kid getting a new toy. She actually squealed in delight.

Squealed.

"Oh, darling. We've been waiting for this moment for so long. I can't tell you how excited we are."

I have to admit, I was feeling the tension, too. I moved over to my mom, grasping her hands in mine. The fervor was palpable.

"Me too! *Thank you!* Thank you both so much for deciding to come. Those assholes aren't gonna break up *this* family, are they?"

"No, son," my dad chimed in, joining us. "No, they aren't."

He clapped me on my back and went over to our small pantry which was just off the kitchen. He pulled the sliding door open, allowing a young woman to step out. She was dressed in an old green hospital gown.

"Garrison, this is your sister, Gilly. She's been living at the sanitarium since before you were born, but she's home now. We can finally all be together."

I stared, mouth agape, at this intruder. She did resemble my mom, it was hard to deny. But her *eyes*. Her eyelids were scarred and her face was a canvas, blank and emotionless.

"What...what is this?" I asked to no one in particular.

Mom spoke first.

"Gilly was born before you, dear. When she started acting out, I'd say around four years old, the government came and fixed her for us. After you were born, we didn't want her to scare you away, so we put her in the sanitarium."

Dad took over from there.

"But now that you've confided your plans to us, we were able to call the doctor and the police. They can fix you too, and we can finally all be together, just like you wanted."

I didn't know what to think. Or feel. Or do. I stood there, looking dumbfounded. Gilly took a hesitant step toward me, and I recoiled.

"She's your sister, son. Don't be afraid."

She looked fairly normal for a girl about twenty; blonde hair, pale skin, average height. But she still wore the sanitarium gown, half of it practically sliding off of her right shoulder in a pathetic, droopy way. Her hair was disheveled and her feet were dirty and bare. When she opened her mouth to speak, what came out made me want to cringe even more.

"Gullah! Ba-ba bra-da!" she barked and drooled and spat all at once. I looked at my parents with disdain.

"You did this to her? *On purpose?*"

"Well," Dad explained, "the surgical technique has improved since then. You'd be amazed how quickly you'll recover, and your speech will be much better than hers."

My mom interjected.

"Speaking of which, they should be pulling into our drive in the next few minutes. Isn't it great, son? We really *can* be together once and for all."

Without missing a beat, I grabbed the keys to my truck and bolted for the front door. Just as I jammed the key into the ignition,

I saw the lights and heard the sirens coming down the block. I threw the beast into reverse and then gunned down on the gas pedal as hard as I could. I wanted as much distance between those monsters and me as I could possibly get.

But they were fast. They had been chasing people down for years and they were good at it. Within the first mile, they had me cornered between a garbage heap and a storage shed. I scuttled out of the passenger door and snaked my way across the field behind the dump. That's where I'm hiding now, underneath a pile of decomposing corpses on the far side of the city dump. I've been here for three days as of this writing.

I'm pretty much against cannibalism, but desperate times, you know? The only thing that differentiates me from these decaying bodies, beside the fact that I'm breathing and they aren't, is that I still have a chance to make it out of here. It's not a big chance, and to be honest, it's not very likely since I can hear them rummaging through the carcasses as I write this. But it's something, and I have to hang on to that belief. If I don't have that, I'll go insane.

FLESH AND BLOOD

Jim Bansky's hands trembled. His eyelid twitched. His breaths grew shallow the longer he stood witness to the unspeakable. A cold rain had just begun but was already soaking into the partially dug graves. Dirt gave way to mud, which in turn gave way to streaks of thin rivers which flowed into the oblong abysses. Overhead, the sky was still debating between various hues of orange, pink and purple; which cloak would best cover the dead?

Jim's blue windbreaker flapped behind him as the wind picked up, but he barely noticed. His concentration was on the task at hand -- the mounds of fresh earth piled up next to the three waiting coffins. Between the dirt, the caskets, and the unforgiving weather, he felt surrounded and suffocated. *A morbid game of ring around the rosy.*

Something between a cough and a laugh escaped his lips, making him painfully aware of his solitude. The noise echoed off the grave markers. He shuddered, blinking the raindrops out of his eyes, and raised his hand to wipe the incessant wetness from his face.

After barely surviving on unemployment over the past fifteen months, Jim was grateful to have a job, even one such as this. Sheer luck and buying a beer for the right guy at the right time was the only thing that had kept him from being homeless. After bending his new buddy's ear about his recent string of bad relationships, lost jobs and D.U.I.'s, his drinking pal offered to make a call and set up an interview at the same place he worked. The next thing Jim knew, he was hired on to the night shift maintenance crew, aka gravedigger, over at the old Greer Cemetery.

Jim's new boss, Gary Nelson, was an asshole. According to the rest of the crew, he always had been and probably always would be. During his first week on the job, the other guys warned Jim not to leave shovels and tarps on the grounds. But the worst offense was staying late, an excuse some of the men used to score a bit of overtime. Jim heeded all the advice from the old-timers; men who had worked there for over ten years, eighteen in a few cases. It was a lifetime compared to his measly few days.

On this particular evening, he was assigned to do all the grave fills alone. When Jim asked why they wouldn't stick around to help out, they just laughed. One of them said it was like a rite of passage. Another slapped him on his back and said he wouldn't be considered a *real* gravedigger if he couldn't be out there alone among the dead.

"You gotta face 'em on their own turf. Think of it as a college frat. This is hell week. And if you *can't* do it, or worse yet, *won't* do it, then maybe you ought to think about looking for another job."

The idea of being out of work again was horrifying. He had already lived in a run-down motel, paying twenty-five bucks a week only to fight off multi-legged critters over a moldy sandwich he swiped from the local gas station. There was no way in hell he was going back to that life.

Once he snagged *this* job, he promised himself that he would do whatever it took to keep it, and if that meant slogging through a few hazing rituals from a bunch of good ol' boys, so be it. The money was decent and if he stayed long enough, he could afford to move into a clean place in a few months. *What's a few weeks of bullshit one way or the other?*

Three caskets rested next to the half dug graves, as if biding their time. Jim was hoping to finish with the burials before sunset, but the last mourners lingered far longer than expected. Now that the weather was being uncooperative, he knew he would be there long after his scheduled shift. It would be dark by the time he was through. *Cold. Wet. Black.*

Each shovelful of dirt landed with an unsettling thud. He worked faster, glancing toward the setting sun. *What was that old rule his grandfather taught him? Hold your hand between the earth and the sun and count each finger as fifteen minutes.* Supposedly, that's how much daylight was left.

Jim held his hand up as if to block out the last remnants of the day. Only one finger separated the earth from the sun. That meant he had fifteen minutes. Nine hundred seconds stood between the bright world of the living and the dark grasp of the dead and the decayed.

He dug and dumped mud carelessly, half of his efforts missing the pile and falling back down into the hole with him. The drizzle turned to a steady rain, soaking through his jacket and plastering his light blond hair to his head. Each shovelful was heavier than the one before, slowing his progress to a pathetic crawl. A large cloud moved in and covered what was left of the sun.

"Fuck," Jim whispered.

Sweat mixed with the rainwater and coated his body. He grabbed for his handkerchief out of habit. The sopping blue square did little to dry his face, but he rubbed it over his eyes and mouth anyway. Just executing the familiar motion was a momentary comfort to the forty-year-old man who looked as if he was pushing seventy.

He was about to take another stab at the unruly soil when he heard a noise.

"No. I still have time. It hasn't been fifteen minutes yet," he muttered. The attempts to calm nerves that could not be soothed were indeed, futile.

Jim whistled tunelessly; anything to cover the unbearable murmurs that whispered to him from the graves. The shovel was so caked with mud that using it was proving pointless, so he dropped to his knees and began raking at the soil with his bare hands, one fistful after the other, throwing them every which way as fast as he could.

The manual labor got the better of him. Jim was exhausted in a matter of minutes. He put his hands on his knees and tried to catch his breath. When he tried to get his footing, he stumbled backwards, tripping over the shovel. He hit his head against the hard clay mud on the side of the empty grave, which promptly knocked him out cold.

Avery Addleson's eyes flew open, throwing him into a fragmented reality. The last thing he could recall with any clarity was driving down Western Boulevard on a Thursday night. He thought he remembered the roads being slick that evening, but he wasn't sure. Quick flashes of a semi-truck surrounded by flying pieces of machinery whirled around in his mind, but none of it made much sense.

He raised his hand up to his face. As he rubbed his cheek, a patch of mottled skin sloughed off, slipped down his neck and came to rest on the shoulder of his suit coat. While his eyes adjusted to the embryonic darkness, Avery took the opportunity to relieve himself from an enormously irritating gas bubble. Wetness pooled around his torso and seeped out through his clothing.

He thought he had heard a consistent *thud, thud, thud* that seemed to resonate through his body. But when the noise stopped, there was nothing but dead silence to match the impenetrable darkness.

He moved both his hands up near his chest and pushed forward. There was a soft layer of billowy satin in front of him. He pushed harder. When nothing budged, he pounded against the silky material until he felt his right elbow give way. The two bones of his forearm had punctured through his skin and were now jutting out behind him. He felt nothing.

His attempt at bending his knees didn't go any better. They were also blocked by some confounding wall in his path. He turned onto his side within the tight confines and tried again. There was just a hint of available space, enough to give Avery the momentum he needed. As he adjusted his position, the scalp on his skull did not turn with him.

Garnering what strength he could, he beat against satin wall. By some miracle, the lid popped apart from the rest of the coffin. Mud slid over the sides and settled down around the space between the walls of the grave and the casket. He thrust his arms forward, one more than the other, forcing the lid to crack, split apart, and open itself to the world.

A gentle rain fell on his face -- what was left of it. He stared wide-eyed into the dark sky; the innate reflex to blink was absent. Lying quietly in the moment allowed Avery to shuffle through images in his mind -- sitting with his wife, Cora, on a sandy blanket at Turtle Beach; running near the ocean with his little brother on the 4th of July; discovering a starfish for the first time.

Nothing about these memories elicited tears or smiles. It was as if Avery was watching a movie about someone else's life. He allowed the random pictures to come, linger for a while, and drift away.

He heard someone mutter, then curse, and had a sudden urge to investigate. The need drove him up and out of his coffin. He grasped the sides and forced his body to rise. Sunken eyes bounced around in their sockets. He shifted his weight from one leg to the other as liquid goo dripped down like stringy ropes from his chest and torso, mixing with the clean patter of the rain. He lifted his face to the sky and let out a burdensome moan. Bubbly, rancid froth dribbled from the corners of his mouth. He wiped it away, along with the skin and tissue surrounding it. Avery began to climb up and out of his tomb, jamming one foot and one hand at a time into the muddy walls.

Jim sat up, still somewhat dazed. The tumble had really done a number on him. As he was coming to, it felt as if his brain had bounced around inside his skull a little *too* hard. He checked his watch. 7:04. The sun had set long ago. There would have been nothing better than to scuttle out of there, take a shower, and have a beer, but there was still work to do. If Gary Nelson happened to drive by and spy dirt mounds and cemetery equipment out at this hour, there would be hell to pay.

He rubbed his head where it had angrily collided with the earth. No blood - a good sign. He scrambled to his feet and hoisted himself out of the hole. He rolled onto the matted, wet grass and stepped carefully around the open grave. He eyed the three waiting caskets with caution and thought he heard rustling in the distance.

"I can hear you assholes. Either come out from hiding and help me finish this shit or go home already."

An eerie moan wisped through the night air and caught Jim's ear. He squinted through the mist and saw the outline of a man. The figure plodded toward him slowly, arms hanging straight down. Jim stood his ground. He extended his own arms in front of him and placed his crossed hands directly on top of the shovel's handle. He would put up with their shit in order to keep his job, but he could still tell them to go to hell.

It was difficult for Avery to make sense of what he was seeing -- old, broken moss- covered stones etched with names and dates, scattered wreaths, wilted flowers, family trinkets. Instinctively, he rubbed his eyes. His right eyeball had dropped down just below his eye socket and was aimlessly floating around behind his cheekbone. Nevertheless, he kept rubbing in a desperate attempt to locate a path through the grounds. Walking was hard enough, but maneuvering around headstones and grave markers was proving to be more than frustrating.

Images and questions bombarded the shreds of his brain. *Where was he? Why would he be in a graveyard? Shattered glass and blood-covered nurses.* He had a penetrating desire to find the answers, to find someone who could help him understand what was happening. He stumbled toward the sound of a man cursing. He had no preconceived notion of what to do or what to say, but the instinct to seek out another human was too strong. He was unable to turn away.

As the distance between the two men lessened, Jim continued to taunt the intruder who he believed was a prank playing co-worker.

"Come on, you dicks. You think it's so funny to harass the new guy? Well, fuck you. I can take a lot more than you think."

Avery trudged forward. With his one eye fixed on the landscape ahead of him, he could see a man resting his hands on an implement. This man was cursing and challenging him to come closer -- to put up or shut up. Avery heard other words but the meanings were lost on him.

When the pair was fifteen feet from each other, the cursing man's reaction changed from anger and confrontation to horror and panic. The pitch of his screams slid from gruff to shrill.

By the time Avery was ten feet away, the man's eyes practically bulged from his head. The wooden implement he was leaning on fell next to him, splattering mud in every direction.

At six feet away, the man went silent. He stood, motionless, hands covering his mouth which had frozen into a silent scream. In the next few seconds, Avery stood within arm's distance of the man who had been in the process of digging his family's graves.

Jim's brain screamed inside his skull. He wanted to shut his eyes and block out this hideousness standing in front of him, but he was too afraid. What if, upon opening them up again, he saw something even worse?

Avery took another step forward as his eye focused on Jim's face. There was an overlying sense of familiarity coming from this man whose stillness was almost palpable. The eye drifted slowly over the man's features; his hair, his eyes, his nose. Another step brought them within inches of one another. Now it was Avery's turn to pause and take in the vision which stood before him. Pieces of recognition sparked across the few neurons left in his brain.

Avery's own hair was still somewhat short from his time in the military. *This* man's hair was long, stringy, and dirty.

Avery recalled that his own eyes were blue. *This* man's eyes were hazel, surrounded by bloodshot whites.

Avery had a Roman nose with the high prominent bridge. *This* man had a rather disconcerting protuberant. It was red and bulbous and lined with highways of purple veins shooting in all directions; a drinker's nose.

A granule of memory flashed from somewhere beyond Avery's comprehension. Something about that connection troubled him. He moved closer, affixing his eye on Jim's face.

What was it about this man that stirred a sense of recognition in him? Avery opened his mouth to speak, but his jaw's hinge no longer had the tension it needed to stay connected. Instead of any vocalization, Avery's mandible popped out and hung downward precariously, still attached by ribbons of skin and sinew.

Jim's hands flew up in front of his face, defending the remaining space between them. He shrieked. His eyes were wide and he thought he would go mad. There *was* recognition in this moment, but it came from Jim *first*.

Avery Addleson was the man Jim ran off the road and killed, the night before he was fired from his last job.

The top half of the three waiting caskets flew open. Avery and Jim turned their heads toward the sudden display as Jim began an endless scream in which nothing or no one could assuage.

When Avery's single eye came to rest upon the upper bodies of the three corpses, the most infinitesimal glimmer of recognition passed across what remained of his face.

A woman and two children.

Didn't he have a wife and two kids? A wife that suffered from depression and at times was so despondent, that she spoke of killing herself and their kids if he ever left them. It had been nearly eighteen months since he remembered seeing them. She managed to last a year and a half without him.

Jim dropped to his knees, cowering in the mud, squeezing his eyes shut. For the briefest of moments he let himself believe it was a dream. Any minute now, his alarm would ring and the daily routine would begin again; the shower, the drive to work, the asinine assignments from the boss, griping and bellyaching with the rest of the guys. Two more weeks of scheduled bullshit and the month would be punctuated by another paycheck. *No animated corpses. No coffins exposing their newly dead. No ghoulish psychopath whose body was literally falling apart, limbs hanging on by threadbare tendons and whose jaw was affixed in an eternal scream.*

Avery reached out and grabbed Jim by his hair, pulling him to his feet. Jim was paralyzed with fear. He tried to cover his face with his hands, but Avery knocked them away and put his thumbs on top of Jim's eyelids.

Jim felt the unwelcoming jab on his eyes, lifting his lids, coercing him to face the ugly truth which stood before him. As he jerked himself backwards, Avery grabbed both his arms and pulled in the opposite directions. His unearthly strength forced Jim's arms out of their sockets. Blood gushed wildly from the gaping holes as he fell to the ground, convulsing spasmodically.

Avery gripped Jim's legs, tearing flesh away from bone. In a final coup de grace, Avery clasped Jim's head between his skinless hands, twisting one way and then the other, until the snap reverberated through Jim's torso.

Lumbering back and forth between the partially open caskets, Avery distributed Jim's dismantled body between the woman and the two children. Once he had finished, the lids closed, locking themselves shut. Avery stumbled back to his own grave and lay quietly as layers of wet earth converged over his tomb.

The cemetery was still. The light rain covered everything in a glistening shimmer under the moonlight. A shovel leaned against a headstone, waiting to be found by the morning crew. Three caskets sat near three partially dug graves.

Gary Nelson would walk the grounds as he did at the start of every morning shift. He would find the job site in a state of disarray and chaos which would cause him to curse out his newest hire. When Gary would return to his office, he would make a note to himself to give that sonofabitch a written warning.

Meanwhile, Avery's skeletal hand gripped a large clump of Jim's stringy hair as both corpse and disembodied head shared the similar expression of a cavernous, screaming maw.

BOOKWORM

The basement of the Ogden Public Library hadn't been touched by human hands for over eight years. Discarded furniture, musty books, Encyclopedia Britannica runs from the 1960s, and long lost office supplies filled the decrepit room. Four ancient electrical sockets hung mockingly from each of the corners. The bulbs blew out years ago and had fallen to the unforgiving cement floor. Their shattered bodies lay exactly where they had dropped; almost a decade of dust and grit covered the shards like earth covering a forgotten tomb. Everything was wrapped in a blanket of grey. Specks of asbestos rested among strands of cobwebs.

The handful of staff that worked at Ogden had long ago dismissed the idea of sorting through the disorganized clutter which lay below their new building like a rotting corpse. When the old building was razed, the new structure was built on top of the basement. It was assumed that clearing out the old place would eventually happen. But as time passed, the thought of purposefully descending those stairs into the abyss became unfathomable.

The new library proved to be quite a boost for the town of Ogden. Contemporary seating replaced the worn and damaged chairs. New computers were installed. A sleek coral colored vinyl floor replaced the old, ratty green shag carpeting from the 1970s. The hallways and walls were painted, and the three librarians added their own touches by creating brightly colored bulletin boards full of updated information as well as news about exciting reading programs targeting all age groups.

The community returned in droves. All of the upgrades and changes spurred a restored interest in literary events and kids programming. No one entertained a single thought about the basement anymore. However, in light of the growing number of visitors, the town council decided to hire a library administrator. There hadn't been a need for such a position in years, but everyone agreed that the times were indeed changing, and with such change, an administrator was needed at the helm again.

Sheryl Norbutt arrived in September. She stood six feet tall, without heels, and wore a hideous pantsuit that screamed love for all things paisley. Her first task, beside for meeting with Jo, Reza, and Audrey, the three librarians who would be reporting to her, was to demand her office door stay closed.

"The last thing I want is to be bothered with petty daily demands. That's what you three were hired for," she said.

The three librarians immediately went online to find out what they could about their new dictator. They didn't like or appreciate having someone over them after all these years of being independent.

Ms. Norbutt had apparently been relieved of her duties from two previous positions as Head Librarian. No specific reasons were given. Legally they couldn't be, but the terminology used was off-putting. Phrases such as 'professional objections' and 'procedural rifts between her and others' were the only evidence of trouble they could glean from their searches.

They concluded that Sheryl planned to run Ogden Public in a strictly dictatorial manner, leaving them out to dry. In their minds, this woman was not going to be told *what* or *how* to do anything, regardless of their years of experience and credibility. To her, they were simply three small-town librarians with a handful of office workers in tow.

"They never give very detailed information, do they?" Reza said. Jo and Audrey sat on either side of her, silently reading from the computer screen.

"Well, that would open a whole can of legal worms, you know. Maybe we can call around to some of those places and find out what *really* happened," Audrey suggested.

Jo started laughing.

"What? What's funny about that?" Audrey asked.

"I can picture these tiny inchworms carrying law diplomas in their mouths," Jo giggled. Reza playfully pushed Jo, causing her to guffaw and snort. The women laughed about the ridiculous image and their concerns about their new boss had faded for a fleeting moment.

After a week of secretive phone calls and emails to previous employers and former co-workers, Reza, Jo, and Audrey met for lunch at a sandwich shop two blocks from the library. The wind had picked up over the past hour. It had become so blustery that Jo could barely hang on to the door's handle. A swirl of loose papers gathered speed and tumbled down the street, catching Reza's eye for a split second as she helped pull the door closed behind them.

"My goodness! If we were closer to the ocean, I'd swear we'd be in for a hurricane," Audrey said, digging through her purse for a hairbrush.

"I'll say," Jo added. "I saw on the news this morning that we're in for some pretty bad storms over the next few days. I just hope the leaks in my roof don't start up again."

"Didn't you get that looked at last year? I thought you had a man patch that up."

"Yeah, he came out to give me an estimate, but when he told me how much it was going to cost, I told him that I was going to buy a big bucket instead and save the money!"

The women laughed, took their coats off, and converged on a corner table out of earshot from the other customers.

"Audrey, would you mind staying here to watch our things? We'll order for you, okay?"

"Sure. Here's a ten," she agreed. "And Jo, whatever's leftover, I'm donating to your bucket fund." Jo took the bill and the women laughed again.

By the time their meals arrived, the trio was deeply entrenched in their conversation about Sheryl Norbutt and her elusive past. In spite of all their best efforts, no one had discovered anything more heinous than what they already knew -- that Sheryl had been re-lieved of her duties at two former employers. Even their attempts to contact past co-workers came up short. The few remaining employees had been rather dismissive of the librarians' inquiries. Most of them had simply replied *'no comment'*.

"It doesn't make a lot of sense," Audrey surmised. "She's got to be, what, in her early 50s at least? If she's worked in libraries for all those years, how come we can't find a single person that's willing to share any inside information on this woman?"

"Exactly. There's got to be something we're overlooking, some-thing that we're missing. Have either one of you contacted the town council? Maybe they could clue us in."

"No, that's a dead end," Jo said. "I've called a couple of my neigh-bors that had been on the council before, but they wouldn't say any-thing. Apparently, they could get in trouble for discussing the hiring process. And, you know, I didn't want to push."

Audrey and Reza nodded. Curiosity was one thing, but jeop-ardizing friends and neighbors was completely another. It wasn't a line the women were willing to cross. Their conversation casually drifted to Jo's leaky roof and Audrey's son's cross country meets. By the meal's end, they had all agreed how wonderful the food was, even though the prices had risen over the past year.

The women bundled up and headed down the street toward the library. As they approached the back door of the building, a crack of lightning and groan of thunder ripped through the sky. An angry rain started to fall.

"...and I won't hear another word about it, Doug. I need that funding for my director's budget and I'm not about to take second place to the VFW. When you hired me, you specifically said that you wanted..."

Sheryl Norbutt paused to peer over the top of her glasses. Audrey stood in the office doorway, her coat partially unbuttoned and a wool hat in her hand.

"Sorry, Sheryl. I guess this is a bad time, huh?" Audrey grimaced.

"Doug, let me call you back. It looks like I have to rescue one of our librarians."

Audrey feigned a smile. She listened to Sheryl cackle into the receiver. *Probably some inside joke at her expense no doubt,* she thought. *Sheryl Norbutt was a real bitch.*

"Okay, Audrey, where's the fire?"

"Well, actually, I was just coming to talk to you about the email you sent this morning. The one asking if anyone was interested in helping out with a special project. I wanted to throw *my* hat in, if you still need a hand." She held up her hat, hoping the reference might get a laugh. It didn't.

Sheryl stared at the librarian with a blank expression. After an uncomfortable extra moment passed, she blinked.

"Good. Jo offered her help as well. It'll be much easier to have *two* sets of hands digging into that mess this weekend instead of one. If you start early enough, I'll bet the two of you can have that basement cleared out in no time."

"The *basement*? You want *us* to clean the basement? You know, there's a lot of furniture down there. *Heavy* furniture. You're not going to be there to help us?"

"That, my dear worker bee, is the difference between librarians and administrators. The town pays *me* to do the thinking and planning, and *you* to execute those plans. I assume you have keys to the building?"

Audrey nodded.

"Perfect. I'd advise you to bring a flashlight or two. I hear it's pretty dark down there."

"Hi, sucker number two," Jo chuckled, waving to Audrey as she slid out of her car.

"I can't believe I fell for this. When she told me what I'd be…"

"What *we'd* be doing, you mean."

"Yeah, well, at least we have each other. How did Reza get out of this nasty detail?"

"Ah, grasshopper," Jo said. "It is only the true brown-noser who actually *asks* to be taken advantage of."

"You mean…" Audrey's eyebrows went up.

"Sure. She never volunteered," Jo said.

The women laughed. They promised each other to remind themselves to use that ploy the next time Sheryl sent an email requesting 'help'.

Audrey reached into her coat pocket and pulled out a set of keys. She hadn't used the long, silver one on the plastic-coated ring for quite some time. Both women stopped short of the stairwell that led down to the basement door.

"Can I tell you something before we go down there?"

""Sure. What is it?" Audrey asked.

"I saw a severed head down here a long time ago."

The following Monday morning, Sheryl Norbutt burst into Reza's office precisely at 8:02. The sudden jolt started a cascade of unpleasant events beginning with startling the librarian and ending with hot coffee being splattered all over her desk and down the front of her new red blouse.

"Oh, for the love of …" Reza spat. She shot Sheryl a dirty look.

"Where's Audrey? She's late. Jo left me a message and said she's on her way, but I can't get a hold of Audrey. The three of you hang out together. Where is she?"

"How in the world should I know? I'm not her keeper. And we don't all hang out together. I wasn't even in town this weekend," she said, dabbing a Kleenex against the shirt stain. "Maybe she's sick and hasn't called in yet. That's certainly possible."

Sheryl sputtered and turned on her heels, leaving Reza to tend to her wardrobe and minor scalds.

"Opening the goddamn building is *not my job,* people. That duty is the responsibility of the librarians," she yelled to no one in particular.

As Sheryl approached the front doors of the building, she saw Jo on the other side of the glass, fumbling around in her purse for her own set of keys. Sheryl turned the lock and held the door open. "Get in here, Jo. You're late."

"I know, I know. I'm really sorry about that. I was trying to get a hold of Audrey. I haven't heard from her since we cleaned out the basement."

"What do you mean?"

"Well, we finished cleaning and were heading to our cars, but she said she forgot something and she'd be right out. I offered to wait for her, but she told me to go on home, that she would lock up. I tried to reach her this morning so we could drive in together, but there was no answer."

"Did you check the basement?"

"No."

"Well, it's a long shot, but there might be a clue. Look, stay here and watch the front desk. Reza's in the back if things get busy."

"Why don't I ask Reza to come out front and I'll go with you? After spending all of Saturday down there, I know my way around pretty well," Jo offered. It was a small olive branch to make amends for her tardiness.

"That sounds reasonable."

With Reza watching the front desk, Jo and Sheryl were free to search the basement. Jo had grabbed a flashlight from her office and Sheryl took her coat. Together, they walked in silence to the stairway, and then down, step by step, heels clicking almost in unison. Sheryl undid the lock and pulled the heavy steel door open, allowing Jo to walk into the darkness ahead of her. The metal slab slammed shut behind them.

"Okay Jo, where's the light switch?"

Jo didn't answer.

"Jo, turn the light on now. I'm serious."

No response.

"Dammit, Jo. Stop fooling around. If you're not going to turn them on, at least turn on the flashlight. Or give it to *me*."

Sheryl fumbled around in the dark for the switch, but never having even seen the layout of the basement, she was at a complete disadvantage. One bulb sizzled to life as Jo flipped the switch. It cast an eerie pall in one corner of the room.

"Jo, I don't like this. You're really starting to make me--" Sheryl started, but was cut off by an unknown voice from another corner of the room.

"Can I tell you something?"

"Jo? Audrey? Is that you?"

"I saw a severed head down here once. And I know who put it there."

"Damn it. Stop this nonsense. Stop playing games."

"Help me...help...me...please. I need help."

"Audrey, is that you? Are you down here? Where are you? I can't see."

"Please. I need your help," the disembodied voice cried out again. Sheryl cocked her head to one side as she tried to navigate her way.

Jo turned off the corner light in order to disorient her boss. Sheryl held her hands out, taking one small step at a time. Without any guidance from Jo or the flashlight, Sheryl eventually made her way into one of the far corners of the basement. She called out again, her voice cracking with desperation.

"Jo? For the love of Pete, would you answer me already?"

In the next moment, she felt two pairs of hands guiding her gently into a chair. She felt the seat tilt, just like the La-Z-Boy recliner she had at home. Her head went back, her feet lifted up, and a sudden beam from Jo's flashlight blinded her.

A hundred year old board sheer had been wedged up against the head of the recliner. An experienced library worker like Sheryl knew immediately what this object was capable of – this four foot paper cutter with a sharp, thick blade on its swing handle. It had been covered by a large beige tarp which currently sat in a crumpled ball next to Jo's feet. The large cast iron workhorse brandished a gleaming, three-foot scythe with a bulbous handle on one end and a solid round counterweight on the other.

Sheryl gasped, horrified by her proximity to the blade, but was more surprised to feel the second pair of hands pressed against her shoulders.

"You know what, Sheryl? You were right about one thing. It *was* good that there were *two* of us here on Saturday. This thing would have been a real monster to move alone, especially here in the dark," Audrey said.

Audrey hoisted Sheryl up just over the top of the recliner by her shoulders, placed her head squarely on the wooden platform, and immediately restrained it with the clamp bar. Jo released the counterweight's pedal which freed the blade and sent it plummeting toward Sheryl's throat. There was a split-second of a guttural scream before she went silent.

"They don't make them like this anymore, huh?" Audrey laughed. She raised the steel cleaver from the bloody mess.

"Are you referring to the board sheer or library administrators?" Jo quipped as she grabbed a rag off of the floor.

"Does it matter?" Audrey said, taking the flashlight from Jo. She needed to put the new light bulbs back in the ceiling sockets.

"I guess you really *did* see a severed head down here, huh?"

"You mean *two*, don't you?"

The two women laughed and got to work. There was still a lot of cleaning to do in the basement.

TRAIL BLAZERS

"Hey, Dan, we're all set. I just got off the phone with the tour guide and they're holding a spot for us. We're down for the 28th."

"That's great, Larry. Thanks for taking care of it, man. I have always wanted to do this. I am so psyched to finally get into the rainforest."

"Yeah, no shit. Make sure you bring your camera this time. I don't want to get there and have to buy those cheap-ass ones from a lousy drugstore like we did in Denmark."

"Alright. But you know you don't have to depend on my top of the line equipment. You can buy your own," Dan laughed.

"Just think of it this way. Ted and I are living vicariously through your expensive photography hobby."

"Bullshit."

"See you soon, man."

Larry Combs, Dan Ivers, and Ted O'Hanion had shared a love of hiking since their college days. The three business majors headed out to any trailhead they could find almost every weekend during their junior and senior years. They especially loved exploring areas 'off the beaten path' – the more desolate and unknown, the better.

Their escapades didn't take them very far from home in the early days since money was tight, but after graduation and the procurement of well-paying jobs, they were able to do some serious traveling. They had visited Wales, Mongolia, Denmark, and Australia, and had plans to see the Fjords of Norway at some point in the not too distant future.

Now with wives in tow, they were even more determined to continue with their travels. Ted and Dan wanted to share their love for hiking with their spouses, to have the bonding experience become all inclusive. Larry went so far as to say that if and when any of them had kids, arrangements would have to be made. They were going to continue these ventures into the wilderness, come hell or high chairs.

The destination for their latest trip was to be in the jungles of Peru. None of the men had been there before, but the thought of experiencing the rainforest couldn't have been more appealing. Larry's wife had to stay home with her ailing mother, but the other two wives were completely on board. They weren't seasoned travelers like their husbands, but both Heather O'Hanion and Dana Ivers were looking forward to the unconventional adventure.

"What the hell do you mean we don't have a guide for tomorrow? I signed up for this trip months ago. Five people for the Rainforest Day Tour on September 28th," Larry said.

He pointed his chubby finger at an underlined confirmation number written on a wrinkly piece of lined yellow paper. His ruddy face was outlined by beads of sweat despite the overworked ceiling fan. He locked eyes with the desk clerk and had no intention of letting go.

"Larry, take it easy, man. We can figure out a way around this," Dan said, placing a hand on Larry's arm.

"No man, this is bullshit. We're not going to be stuck in some godforsaken area of Peru without a fuckin' plan. We can't get a refund for this, you know. We paid our money back in June; that was supposed to be our contract with this outfit."

Larry glared at the clerk, ready to do battle.

"Sir, I will tell you again. I am sorry for your troubles, but the guide for *that particular* trip is ill. There are no other qualified staff members available, but I would be happy to reschedule your party for another time."

"Come on, Larry, we can do another one. Let's look at what else they have," Dan said. He was embarrassed and desperate to alleviate the escalating situation. Ted and the two women nodded in agreement. If there was one troubling thing about Larry, it was his hair-trigger temper.

"I don't know..." Larry grumbled. The clerk handed Larry a brochure. Reluctantly, he took it and eyed Ted and Dan. "I've really been counting on this, you know. We *all* have, haven't we? This was the main purpose of our trip and now we're totally screwed."

"Hey, think of it this way," Heather spoke up. "Dana and I haven't been anywhere like this in our lives. *Any* hike we do is going to be amazing, right?" She eyed Dana for confirmation.

"Heather's right. I mean, we are in fuckin' *Peru*. How cool is that?"

"Fine," Larry conceded.

The clerk offered copies of the brochure to the rest of the group. After a brief discussion, they came to a consensus and agreed to let Larry take care of the arrangements. The two couples left the shop and waited by their rental car. Larry turned back to the clerk and pulled out his wallet before signing everyone up for the new hiking tour.

"This should take care of things, right?" He slipped the clerk some cash and whispered in the man's ear. The man slid the money across the counter and right into his hip pocket. A hint of a smile crept over his face.

"It will more than take care of things, sir. Leave the details to me."

Larry took the new confirmation sheet and corresponding maps, tucked them underneath his arm, and walked out under the day's glaring sun to meet his friends.

Ted O'Hanion was showered, dressed, and packed for the sunrise hike long before his wife had even thought about opening an eye from her deep slumber. He puttered around the motel room, playing with the remote and fussing in the bathroom until Heather reminded him that she had forty minutes left until her alarm was scheduled to go off and could he 'please go elsewhere during that time'? He stepped out onto the balcony and whispered '*goodnight*' toward the lump under the covers before closing the door.

"You get booted out too?" Dan chuckled.

"How'd you guess," Ted smirked and gave an upward nod to Larry, who was standing next to Dan.

"Are we gonna make it by six? What's the story with the women folk, guys?"

"Yeah, it's cool, Larry. It won't take Dana long to get ready."

"Same for Heather. We should be fine. You've got all the papers and everything, right?"

Larry smiled and took a large swig from his 64 ounce coffee mug. He held up the map and papers in his hand. "I got it covered, guys. I promise this is going to be even better than the hike that got fucked up the other day. Trust me."

"Cool," Ted said. "Larry Combs, you don't take any shit from anyone, do you? Not even a pissant clerk in the middle of bumfuck Peru. Good for you, man. The trip is costing us enough as it is."

The three men laughed out loud, just like old times.

Forty-five minutes later, the group loaded up their rental vehicle and headed down to the tour center. They arrived at 5:45am, along with a few other tourists who were busy chatting among themselves in small clusters near the wall of maps and travel guides.

A tall, thin man with a bright yellow name tag around his neck approached Larry and the two couples. He held his hand out as he neared.

"Good morning. My name is Marco and I will be your guide today. I see you are registered for the Tropical Sunrise Tour, yes? And I see you have your maps already, too. Great. As we drive to the trail head, I'll cover some rules that I need you to follow. Since we are a small group, we should be able to cover a great deal of ground in the three hours that we have. Now, if everyone is ready, let's head out to my jeep. It's the one with the yellow flag on the hood."

Marco chatted quietly with Heather and Dana while the three men sat in the back reviewing the maps and legends. When not making small talk, Marco pointed out unique flora and shared stories about animals that he had seen on previous hikes. A palpable buzz of excitement vibrated throughout the vehicle as they closed in on their destination.

"Here we are, my friends. Gather your bags and cameras and let's meet right over there, next to that tree," Marco said, pointing at an Aphanda Natalia, a fiber palm tree.

Everyone piled out and grabbed their gear. Marco adjusted his own backpack and joined the group.

"Okay, here's the trail head; this is where we start. Remember, you each have your own map just in case anyone gets separated from the group. Since there's only six of us, I don't think that will be a problem, but it's always good to plan for the unexpected."

"Separated?" Heather piped up. She was rattled by the mere mention of such a thing. "Marco, that isn't even a *possibility*, is it? Getting separated out here? I mean, come on, you have to be pulling our legs or something, right?"

"I assure you, the chance of getting lost out here with an experienced tour guide is very remote. I pull no legs. But, our regulations state that everyone who goes on our hikes has to carry their own map. As we get further into the rainforest, the canopy will create a kind of darkness unlike anything you might have encountered in the states. There are many levels of vegetation and it's easy to become disoriented. Everything can look the same to the untrained eye."

"Yeah, but if you're with us, and you know all the trails around here, we should be fine, right? I mean, I don't know how much good a map like this is going to do me," Heather pressed.

"We'll be fine, Heather. Don't read anything into it. He has to say stuff like that, you know, like a waiver," Ted said. "No one's going to be out here by themselves."

"Yeah, it's fine," Dana added. "We're not going to let you get lost. Just don't wander off to pet the wildlife."

"Okay. Is everyone ready? Let's go," Marco said, leading the small group down a well worn path through a break in the tree line.

Ted, Larry, Dan, Dana, and Heather walked in single file behind their tour guide, silently taking in the wild surroundings. For almost two miles, only the sounds of the rainforest accompanied them: snapping of twigs, rustling of leaves, chirps and caws from species unseen. No one, not even Heather, complained about the oppressive humidity or the increase of muddiness on the trail.

Around the two and a half mile mark, Marco stopped walking and turned to face the group.

"Okay, everyone. Let's take a break. We're almost an hour into it. I also want to remind you to keep drinking. You might not realize it because of all the wetness in the rainforest, but it is possible to become dehydrated. Pretty ironic, huh? Dehydration in a place like this?"

Dana nodded. She was a nurse. She understood.

"I'm going to take a minute or so to relieve myself. Feel free to do the same. Then, we'll continue on for another half hour before heading back. Sound good?"

"Sounds like perfect idea," Larry agreed. "I'm all for a pee break in the action."

Somewhat amused by the crassness of their friend, each of them walked in a separate direction for a moment or two of privacy. A short time later, as the group reconvened, Larry and Dan were already questioning the whereabouts of Marco.

"I don't know, man," Dan shrugged. "We all watched him go over there in that direction. Maybe he's taking a crap instead. That can take a little longer."

"I was under the impression that this break in the action was more of a quick piss, shake it off, an' go kind of thing. I didn't expect him to sit there with a goddamn fuckin' book, you know?"

"Nice language, Larry," Dana scoffed.

"What? You've heard me cuss before."

"Yeah, I know, but Jesus, give the guy a break. So we wait here for a few extra minutes. Why does everything have to happen on *your* schedule? Maybe the rest of us appreciate the break."

"Guys, guys," Ted broke in. "Relax, okay? Let's not get into it. It's too muggy to argue."

"I wasn't arguing," Larry stated. "I was just pointing out the fact that taking your dick out of your pants for a quick piss and shake shouldn't take more than a fucking minute or two, at most." His face was playing host to beads of sweat again. He wiped his forehead with his shirt-tail. "And yes, Dana, I said *fucking*. Grow up and deal with it," he added.

"Hey, dude. Not cool," Dan said, maneuvering himself between his wife and his friend. "Don't even think about starting in with Dana."

"Look, I can't help it if your wife's a prude..."

"Fuck *you*, Larry," Dan yelled and lunged toward him.

Ted and Heather grabbed for Dan before the two men could make contact. Fortunately for everyone, Ted outweighed Dan by a good thirty pounds. Heather was just along for the ride.

"Stop it, you two. Just stop it," Dana demanded. "Marco? *Remember him,* the whole point of this stupid fight? He's not back yet. So instead of fighting with each other, why don't you guys harness all this energy and go look for him?"

"Yeah. She's right. Where the hell is he?" Ted said. "It's been way too long now."

"What should we do? Should we wait? Ted, I'm getting a little nervous," Heather said.

Dan and Dana started calling out together. Ted joined in. He cupped his hands around his mouth and yelled as loud as he could.

"*Marco!!*"

"Guys?" Larry spoke. His face was flush, but not from the heat. He stared down at the floor of the rainforest, his hands jammed deep within his pockets. "Guys. Stop. You don't need to call him. It's...it's okay. He's not missing."

"What do you mean, 'he's not missing'? Did you see where he went?" Dan asked.

"Well, actually..." Larry started. He kept eyeing the ground.

"Spill it, Larry. What the hell is going on here?" Ted demanded.

"Marco split," he whispered. Larry's lips quivered into a perverted smirk. He still refused to make eye contact with anyone in the group.

"Obviously, you're the genius among us. Don't you think we're all painfully aware that Marco is gone?" Dana said, swatting away a buzzing disturbance from landing on her head.

"No, he *really* left. I paid him to leave."

"What? What does that mean?""

"When? When did you pay him? Just now? I didn't see anything. What are you talking about?" Heather asked.

"Back in the office. After all you guys left. When I signed us up for this new hike, I, uh, made special arrangements."

Dana had heard enough. She jumped towards him, fists flying, screaming all the way.

"*What the fuck were you thinking?* Why in God's name would you do something as stupid and irresponsible as that, Larry? What are we supposed to do now? None of us have ever been out here! How in the hell are we supposed to know where to go?"

Larry held his hands out, trying to fend off Dana's wild punches. He was drenched -- sweat-soaked right through his clothes to his skin. His blonde hair stuck to his head like a thin helmet, making his ruddy face appear more angry than terrified.

"I-I can do it," he whimpered. "*I wanted to prove to you guys that I could do it...that I could lead everybody.*"

"That's fuckin' great, man," Ted said. "That's just great. At least we got these maps and a compass, so we can figure this out. But let me tell you one thing, Larry. This is really fucked up, you know that? What made you pull a stunt like this? Jesus, we've been doing this for too long. You know better than to screw around in a new place. Especially somewhere like this."

"As soon as we get back to our room, I'm calling our lawyer and sue the hell out of that tour company. What kind of fly-by-night outfit agrees to this kind of shit? I'm serious, Dana, remind me to get a hold of Mike Biggs, okay? He's going to have a field day with this."

Heather started crying. Ted hugged her and whispered that everything was going to be fine, that he and Dan would be able to get them out of there. She looked at him with puffy, red eyes, wanting to believe in him and hoping he had enough courage for the both of them.

"Larry, you are an idiot. I have put up with you for the sake of my wonderful husband, Dan, but for the life of me, I don't know how you guys are still friends. I have officially had it up to here with you and your bullying and your constant need to prove what a big man you are," Dana paused for a deep breath before continuing.

"I think the fair thing to do is for the rest of us to leave you right here to find your own way back. And of course, you must have realized by now that if Marco *really* left us, like you stupidly *paid* him to do, he probably took the jeep back to the office. Maybe he didn't consider the fact that we need to get *back there* and not just *out of here*. Did *that* cross your mind, you asshole?"

"I can do this," Larry muttered under his breath. His affect became frighteningly deadpan. His voice was flat and a watery glaze coated his eyes.

"Just...follow...me..."

"Hold on. Why don't we look at the maps first, okay, buddy? You're right, we *can* do this, but we have to have a plan first," Ted suggested and moved closer to Larry.

"Just...follow...me..."

Larry turned and started walking in the opposite direction. The others exchanged looks, adjusted their gear and followed, believing that their friend might have other information they didn't know about, possibly more surprises that he had previously arranged. They chose to give him the benefit of the doubt for the time being.

A little over three hours had passed since Marco took off, leaving Larry as a poor excuse for a tour guide. The maps were worthless and the compass was faulty. Larry had seen to that as well. He didn't want any assistance from tour guides or maps or any *pansy-ass shit.* That was the deal with the devil he made when money exchanged hands back at the office.

But now, daylight was fading underneath the tropical canopies and darkness had become the watchword. The humidity was playing havoc with everyone's internal thermostats. After a few more hours of mindless wandering, there was a sense that the forest was starting to awaken. They had heard the squawk of birds and chattering of small mammals since they arrived with Marco hours earlier, but things were different now. They were more sinister.

"Jesus, Larry. Are you sure you know where you're going? We should have been back by now," Dan said. "C'mon, man, let's stop and check the maps again. This isn't right, it's taking too long."

"I can do this. I can get us out."

"Just stop for a minute, okay?" Ted yelled from the rear of the line.

But Larry wouldn't stop. He kept walking through the rainforest and his friends kept following him.

"Stop! *Larry! Wait a minute,*" Dana called out.

He refused.

Ted and Dan raced to the front of the group and stood directly in front of him like a human wall, but Larry simply skirted around them and continued through hanging vines and outstretched branches full of leaves, not even bothering to push them aside as he passed. Ted threw his hands up in the air and pulled the map out of his pocket. Dan was already looking at his, trying to make sense of it, but coming up with nothing. As experienced as they were, neither man could figure out a basic sense of direction from the pages they held.

"Why won't the motherfucker stop?! What's the matter with him?" Ted shouted.

"I don't know," Dan answered. "But in order to figure anything out, we need to stop first. If we just keep walking around aimlessly, we're only digging ourselves further in. Do you think he has any real sense of where we're going?"

"I don't know. Apparently, he made some under the table deals with the tour guides, so who knows? Maybe he does know something we don't. But following him blind like this is bullshit. I'm out of water already."

"Yeah, me too. I think the only way we're going to get a straight answer is to hold him. Like, *physically* hold him."

"I agree, Ted. We're gonna have to do it."

Dan tapped Dana on the shoulder as the four of them continued walking after Larry.

"Dana, we're going to need you and Heather to help with something, okay?"

"Sure. If it has anything to do with stopping, count us in."

The four of them passed information back and forth like an elementary school game of phone tag. As they were deciding who would make the first move, Larry dropped to the forest floor in front of them and crawled under an enormous fallen tree. Once he was clear, he stood up and started walking again.

"Shit," Dan said, dropping to his hands and knees.

There was about a three foot clearance between the bottom of the tree trunk and the floor of the rainforest. How Larry scuttled underneath and out the other side so quickly was a feat unto itself,

Dan thought. But if a guy that size could do it, this should be a piece of cake for everyone else. He began to crawl under the trunk but stopped about six inches prior. His eyes were glued to something hanging from the underside of the tree.

"Jesus."

"He's getting away, man. *Go! Hurry up!* Get under there. We can't go around this thing. It's too long. We'll lose him!" Ted shouted.

"I-I can't. I--" Horror took over Dan's need to stop Larry. "There's something under there. I just can't..."

"Dan, please. Come on, I'll be right behind you," Dana spoke. She got down on all fours and crawled toward the tree trunk but stopped short. She saw what her husband had seen. Dana sprung to her feet. "I am not going under there. Larry can go fuck himself for all I care."

"What?" Heather asked. She saw the fear and repulsion in her friend's eyes.

"Spider."

"Oh, for the love of --" Heather laughed. She loved animals, *all* animals. A silly spider wasn't about to stop their progress. She bent down and approached the tree herself. She turned her head upward to see what could possibly stop two rational adults in their tracks. Her face went pale and she recoiled.

"Heather, not you too," Ted bemoaned.

"It's huge. It has babies..."

"There's no way Larry crawled under that tree without getting some on him. He just didn't care. He was too out of it to care."

Ted bent down and looked. His friends were right. It was the size of a dinner plate not including the legs. It might have been poisonous, but how would they know? Ted looked closely at the fallen tree. It was teeming with babies. They couldn't even scale the thing without certain contact, and if they backtracked now the chance of them locating Larry would fall from slim to none.

Heather screamed. "They're *everywhere!* We have to get out of here!"

The rainforest *had* come alive. Not just with spiders, but with other organisms that crept and crawled and scuttled over every surface, including the ground. It was dark and cool now, the perfect environment for creatures to move and search for a *new* host. And it would be easy enough to find one if a body lingered in one place too long; a little more difficult if a body kept moving. The foursome now understood the dire need *stay in constant motion* even if there was no certainty of finding a way out. Keep moving regardless of the cost.

Just like Larry.

FAMILY REUNION

Jack Wells couldn't have been more excited. He didn't remember the last time he had brought a special lady with him to his family reunion. By this point, he assumed that his relatives had all but given up on the idea of him ever finding the *right* woman.

He was no slouch when it came to dating, however. At 52 years-old, he could still charm the hell out of a girl half his age if he had a mind to do it. Waitresses and shop clerks were constantly slipping him their telephone numbers. Women he met at bars were forever giving him *come hither* looks under the unassuming eyes of their boyfriends or husbands. To say Jack enjoyed a number of sexual conquests in his day would be a modest understatement. But regardless of all this attention, he never found someone *special* enough to bring home to the family.

He was growing tired of the dating scene. Willingness and good looks weren't enough for him anymore. His friends and peers weren't just parents now; they were grandparents. Photos of family vacations, children gathered around Christmas trees, and kids' graduation ceremonies taunted him from co-workers' adjacent cubicles at work. How could he show off his own photographs if he could barely remember the names of the women in them?

Jack wanted to settle down. He wanted someone who could hold their own during a conversation, someone who understood the references to his jokes, someone who grew up with the same music. When his latest hook-up admitted that she had never heard of John Lennon, the reality of his life hit him like a punch to the gut. Remorse and depression began to set in. He believed that his best years were long gone and he'd probably die alone, or worse yet, next to someone who had never seen a rotary dial phone.

Until he met Kim.

Kim Curtis was a fifty-five year old widow who moved into Jack's apartment complex last year around Thanksgiving. He had volunteered to help her move in and do any heavy lifting. She was grateful to have the assistance, especially after Jack turned on the charm. In turn, he found her to be smart, funny, and fiercely independent. It didn't take long for them to become an *exclusive item* at the Brentwood Condos.

As time passed, Jack felt the relationship had gone far beyond the usual tryst. She was the first thing on his mind every morning and the last thing he thought about every night. He couldn't wait to see her, to be in her presence, and share time together. By early summer, he was convinced. She was indeed *the one*. All that was left was for Kim to meet the family.

"Kim, I can't tell you how much you mean to me. You know I've dated other women. I've been pretty transparent about my past. But...but this is different. I can honestly say that you're the most important person in my life. I told Mom that I was bringing you to the reunion and she told me that she was going to talk you up to the rest of the family."

"Oh, Jack, I hope you didn't go overboard. I wouldn't want to end up disappointing anyone," Kim smirked. She picked a lint ball from her skirt and stuffed it in between her seat and the door. "I'm just a regular person like everybody else."

"Well, for one thing, you're a professional woman with an important job. That's pretty special right there."

"I'm an R.N. like thousands of other people."

"I know, I know," he said, placing his hand on her knee. "But to me, everything you do is amazing. I can't wait to show you off to my whole family. What's so wrong about that?"

"Well…thanks. I guess I'm pretty nervous about meeting everyone at once." She blushed and turned her gaze toward the passenger window.

"I just want them to see what a wonderful woman you are. I mean, I want you to be part of the Wells' family." He eased the car onto the shoulder of the road and turned off the engine. In one smooth move, he pulled a tiny box from his shirt pocket and handed it to Kim.

"I don't know what to say."

"Say 'yes'."

A few stray tears fell from her eyes. She wiped them away and looked at Jack.

"Yes! Of course! I love you."

"And I love you, Kim." They kissed and shared an awkward hug over the center console of the car.

"I was hoping that would be your answer."

"For me, that was the only one," she said. "We, uh, better get to the reunion though, huh? Can't keep your family waiting."

It was going to be next to impossible to contain her excitement in front of a bunch of strangers, she thought. *They won't be strangers -- they'll be my family.*

It was a four hour drive to Shilling's Park. Jack had driven the whole way, even though Kim had offered to take the wheel. He dismissed the very idea of it. He said that his energy level was high, *very* high, and if she wanted to help pass the time, she could share more stories about her life. Anything was fair game: early childhood, brooding teenage mishaps, even details about her late husband, who he knew died from cancer, but never pressed her for specifics. Six and a half months of serious dating still allowed plenty of opportunity to discover new things about each other.

Jack pulled the car onto a gravel road and headed toward a large parking lot. There were already a number of cars and campers filling the spaces, but he spotted an empty one close to the playground.

"Well, here we are. Shilling's Park, home to the Wells' summer reunions. And now, if I may, allow me to open your door, take your arm, and escort you down the path to the picnic area, where throngs of admirers are awaiting your arrival." He practically leapt from the driver's side and ran around the front of the car to her door.

"You are too much," Kim laughed. "Sure, by all means. I see that chivalry is alive and kicking in this leg of the family."

She offered her hand to Jack, who bowed, kissed it, and helped her out of her seat. She stood, adjusted her skirt, straightened her top, and fluffed her hair. She hadn't met a suitor's entire family in over thirty years, when she and Russell were first engaged. That image triggered so many fond memories, and yet here she was again, nervously primping as if she was twenty-one years old.

"I can assure you that all the men in my family have exquisite manners and know how to treat a lady. If you'll take my arm? Thanks. You know, I do believe I will be the envy of every man here."

"I sure hope the rest of your family has your sense of humor," she said, playfully slapping his shoulder. They shared a laugh and walked from the parking lot toward the rest of the group. As they neared, they heard a woman shouting.

"Jack's here, everyone!"

"Hello, Mom," Jack beamed, arms open wide for the embrace he knew was coming. "How are you? You sounded wonderful the last time we talked on the phone. I want you to meet Kim, the incredible lady I've been bragging about for the past few months." He stepped aside, allowing the two women to meet.

"How do you do, ma'am? I'm Kim Curtis. Jack has said some very nice things about you."

"Has he now? Well, that's nice of you to say. I'm glad he's found a friend to keep him company for the long car ride. He's a wonderful son, you know. As I get older, it's important for a parent to know that their children have reliable friends they can count on. You and Jack *are* just friends, right? Sometimes, I think my son gets a little carried away about the seriousness of his relationships. Politeness can be mistaken for romantic interest, and Jack was always taught to have good manners, weren't you, son?"

"Absolutely," he agreed, placing a hand on each of the women's shoulders. "And now that my two favorite people in the whole world have met, let me introduce you to the rest of the family."

As they stepped away from Mother Wells, Kim whispered in his ear. "That was kind of a strange greeting, don't you think? I mean, '*just friends*'?"

"Well, she can be a little overprotective. It's the way she's always been."

"I suppose, but it sounded a little...defensive. Doesn't she realize that we're more than...?"

Before they could discuss it further, other family members had gathered and began introducing themselves. She shook hands with cousins, aunts, uncles, and other assorted relatives. After meeting so many people, an uneasy feeling washed over her.

"Please excuse me for a moment." Kim begged off and headed to an empty picnic bench away from the crowd. Jack followed close behind.

"Are you doing okay? You look a little...ill."

"What's going on here, Jack? Is there something you're not telling me?"

"I'm not sure what you're talking about. I know my family's pretty big so I imagine this can feel pretty overwhelming. Why don't you let me get you a drink, okay? You'll feel better after you have something cold."

"Jack," she whispered, "there's something peculiar about your family."

"What are you saying, Kim?"

"There's something wrong. Seriously wrong."

"Look, I'm sorry that you think Mom put you on the spot back there, but I wouldn't give it too much weight. She can be a prickly pear if she thinks another woman is vying for my affections. That's probably all this is – some pangs of jealousy. Now, let me get you that drink, alright?"

Kim didn't want Jack or his family thinking of her as the pro-verbial stick in the mud. She was already nervous and on edge. *Maybe it's true, maybe I am making too much of everything.* And while she didn't feel welcomed by his mother in the slightest, the rest of his relatives seemed approving and kind.

She just found it very strange that most everyone here had something missing -- a hand, an arm, or in a few cases, both legs. *Perhaps it was a genetic disease,* she reasoned. As a nurse, Kim had seen disfigured bodies. In fact, there probably wasn't any kind of physical deformity that would surprise her anymore. Interacting with people who had missing limbs was routine; it was part of her job.

But this was different. *These* people had not returned from a war zone. A few might have been in the military, but certainly not eighty percent of them. Other than high doses of Thalidomide, she could think of no other reason that would explain these kinds of defects. And that would most likely only account for the people born in the late 50s or early 60s, not the multi-generational mutations standing in front of her now.

"You're right. It must just be my nerves or something. I'm sorry. I didn't mean anything by what I said, or asked, or... oh, I don't know," she finally laughed. "I guess I'm acting like a goofy teenager. I just want to make a good impression, that's all."

"Of course. I understand," Jack reassured her. He took her hand and helped her up from the bench. "This is a big day. I'm sure everybody is a little on edge." She smiled and embraced him before kissing his cheek.

"There you are," Mother Wells said. Her fists were firmly braced against her hips giving her the appearance of a teapot ready to whistle. Her short stature and rotund body didn't do her any favors. "Food's getting cold and people are hungry. We held up saying grace for *you*, you know."

"Well, we're right here now, Mom, everything's fine," he placated.

"Come on, everyone," she bellowed. "Time to say grace. The prodigal son is back."

As the group gathered together, Mother Wells thanked the heavens and the angels for this blessing and that bit of good fortune. Jack whispered something to Kim, making her smile. He took her left hand in his right, and then clasped the hand of a cousin with his left. Kim followed suit, holding Jack's hand, giving it a quick squeeze.

An elderly man approached her from the other side and extended his arm. She was still smiling and flirting with Jack as she reached over to take hold of the man's hand. As her fingers began to intertwine with his, she instinctually pulled away. She turned to look at the man whose hand was as clammy and cold as a dead fish. Her eyes darted up from his hand to his arm, over his shoulder, and finally coming to rest on his face. She screamed.

Mother Wells stopped in mid-blather as everyone turned toward Kim. Jack closed his eyes, realizing that things were about to get complicated, and leaned in close to her.

"Just say you saw a spider," he whispered. "Don't say anything else."

"No!" she screamed again, this time directing her astonishment pointedly at Jack. "Something is wrong with this man. *Look at his face!*"

The group unclasped hands and began to circle around Kim.

"Look! Jack, don't you see? This man..." she started.

"That's Uncle Bertrand."

"Well, Uncle Bertrand is in dire need of medical attention. His skin is peeling right off his face. And, my God, look at his hands. His stomach is so distended -- I've never seen anything like this in a living human. We need to get this man to the hospital *now*. I'm sorry to say this in front of everybody here, but your uncle looks like he's been decomposing for a week."

"You are one *hell* of a nurse, Kim Curtis," Mother Wells stated, pushing past other family members with her cane. "As of today, it's been precisely nine days. But I have to give you credit for your guess being so close."

"Nine days? Nine days for what?" Kim sputtered, never once taking her eyes off of the disfigured body wobbling in front of the family.

"Come on, Kim," Jack offered his hand to her. "Let's go for a walk and have a chat, huh? Give everyone a chance to calm down here."

"No. It's my job to help people and this man obviously needs help." She turned to face the man square on. "Sir, can you understand me?"

Uncle Bertrand's lips parted slightly, revealing an uneven row of grey, slime-coated teeth. A maggot slithered out from under his bottom lip. As his smile grew, both lips split open, audibly cracking in the center as they parted. A heavily burdened sigh escaped as he tried to speak. But instead of words, a putrid cloud of intestinal gas wheezed up and out from his throat. He raised an arm to reach for Kim, but as he extended it, there was a detectable click and release in the elbow joint. His forearm dislodged and fell to the ground.

Kim screamed again.

"Jack, is there something you forgot to tell your lady friend here?" Mother Wells scolded.

"*I didn't want to ruin it*," he shouted into his mom's face.

"What's going on? What's happening? Why isn't anyone helping this man?" Kim shrieked and stepped back, distancing herself from the living corpse in front of her.

A female cousin who was clothed in a pale yellow dress and a wide brimmed hat began edging herself toward Kim, holding out both hands in an effort to calm the hysterical woman. As she inched closer to Kim, it became very clear that her wardrobe dated back to the 1940s. The cousin raised her head as if to look Kim square in the eye, except that she had no eyes. Wisps of brittle hair barely hid the fact that she had no skin left on her face at all.

"Jack!" Kim screamed.

"I can't help it if some of them are already dead. It's a *family* reunion. Everyone's always been welcome."

"You're crazy! You're all crazy. What's the matter with you?"

"They'll love you as much as I do. You just have to give it some time."

Kim spun around to face Jack. He stepped toward her, spreading his arms, wanting to embrace his fiancé, but she pushed him away. She thought about running. She thought about screaming. She thought about living alone for the rest of her life.

Instead, she turned to face his entire family as they closed in around her, reaching out to welcome her into their brood.

BLUE

oyce counted to eight again as he walked up and down the rows of sweaty, tired students. Class was just about over and he hoped he hadn't come across as the *easy instructor* again. He was not fond of that label. In fact, having the reputation as 'the old guy' was getting pretty tiresome.

He had always secretly compared himself to the other fitness instructors at Slim Gym. How could he help it? Chronologically, he *was* the oldest. He was also the shortest, the baldest, and the only one married. Although he and his two business partners, Mark and Glenn, owned equal shares of the gym, Boyce felt like a hamster running in a wheel, trying to prove himself time and time again - not just with them but with the students as well.

For five years, Slim Gym provided access to free weights and basic lifting machines for their clients, but was most notably known for the cardio classes. They were sixty minute long, high intensity workouts and were taught four times a day, five days a week. Best of all, their prices were competitive enough to entice the local co-eds away from the campus recreation centers.

Boyce Prior was thirty-five, five feet six, and brandished the beginning of a not-so-discreet comb over. He had married his girlfriend right out of high school and continued following the life script by having three kids as soon as possible. They rescued a dog from the pound, hired the teen next door to mow the lawn and pull weeds, and decorated their home in country gingham. Boyce's wife, Margie, decided early on that her role would be that of housewife. She spent the majority of her day changing diapers, watching daytime soaps, and becoming very familiar with the workers down at Dunk Your Doughnuts.

After years of working dead end jobs, Boyce received a call from Glenn, a family friend, who offered him a business proposition his couldn't refuse.

Boyce missed his healthy lifestyle from the old high school days and longed for some kind of companionship that didn't involve re-caps of *Our Lives and Loves* or *Sesame Street*. Boyce said yes without even consulting Margie. Eight months later, Slim Gym was up and running with the help of Glenn's friend, Mark. Word of mouth spread quickly and in just under two years, Boyce and his partners were in the black.

The three men quickly fell into a routine of visiting the local pub on Thursday nights for happy hour after all the classes were over. It was a chance to talk a little business as well as compare notes about women. Glenn and Mark were in their mid-twenties and could easily have passed for models. Neither man had a hard time finding women who were *willing*.

"Getting dates around here is like shooting fish in a barrel," Mark had once told Boyce.

But he didn't mind. Boyce was happy to be part of this *boy's night out*. He actually looked forward to it since it gave him an excuse to be away from the house and out from Margie's suspicious eyes, all under the guise of doing business. It was the rare occasion that she would call him on those Thursday nights. If she did, it was only to badger him about stopping by the chicken place on his way home and to 'remember the extra fuckin' biscuits this time'.

Bethany Rivers, a young woman from one of the local colleges, had recently joined Slim Gym after seeing a coupon in the school paper. The ad touted fifty percent off the first six months; a deal she couldn't pass up. She had gained the dreaded 'freshman fifteen' during her first, second, and third year in school, but now she was ready to do something about it.

Bethany committed herself to making better food choices -- no more large pepperoni pizzas, no more twenty ounce Cokes, and absolutely no more double stuff Oreos, even if she did toss the cookie part away. Jars of marshmallow Fluff, hidden behind boxes of lime Jell-O like a fortress protecting royalty, also had to be pitched.

However, in order to make a lasting change, Bethany dedicated a portion of her time to regular bouts of exercise. She attended the 6:30pm class four nights a week without fail. When she was allowed, she drove her roommates' car, but the way their moods blew hot and cold, that option wasn't always available. On evenings when they couldn't be convinced, she walked or took the bus.

Three months in, Bethany started seeing results. The weight was coming off and her old clothes were beginning to bag. Before finals week, she indulged herself by buying a new wardrobe. She also decided to stay at school over the summer break. She found a day time job at a local tea shop and kept her evenings free for Slim Gym.

Summer usually meant smaller classes and reduced hours. With a large portion of their clientele coming from the universities and community colleges, there were considerably fewer students hanging around after May. Glenn and Mark decided to take advantage of the hiatus and booked a three week vacation in Florida. They relinquished the reigns of responsibility to Boyce, who never went anywhere anyway. Margie made sure of that.

Ever since she first signed up at Slim Gym, Bethany had admired Boyce, not just as an instructor but as someone who could relate to being the odd-person-out. He was always patient with her while she struggled to do pushups, encouraged her to squeeze out one more sit-up, and was quick with a thumbs-up during squats. Most importantly, he took the time to chat with her (and the others) after class, something Mark and Glenn only did with the *pretty* girls.

By the middle of June, Bethany had developed a full-fledged crush on this married man who was almost fifteen years her senior.

One sweltering July evening, Boyce led a class of seven students through a particularly hellish workout. For some reason, he had a fire in him that night. He pushed himself and his class further than he ever had.

Sweaty, tired, and drained, everyone gathered their water bottles and bags and headed for the door without spending time with the usual after-class chatting session.

Everyone but Bethany.

"That was a pretty crazy class. Are you secretly trying to kill us so you can leave early on Thursdays?" Bethany asked. There was the smallest quiver in her voice. She had never been alone with him, not *really* alone. There was always someone in the locker room or the office. She felt her heart race and her face flush.

"Hey, I never thought of that. I like it," he laughed. "I'll have to try that next Thursday."

"I'll be here. You can count on that."

"Good."

He picked up the mats and jump ropes that were scattered around the room. Bethany placed a few hand weights into a yellow basket. She went to reach for the green ones but he stopped her.

"Just leave those over there. I'll need them for the early class in the morning. The seniors like the five pound weights over the others."

Blue

"Sure," she paused and took a deep breath. "You know, I really like it when you teach the class. You're a lot better than Glenn."

"Thanks, I appreciate that. But don't sell Glenn or Mark short. They know their stuff. They've been doing this a long time, longer than me, actually. You should give them a chance. Try some of their classes if you can."

"Well," Bethany said, "maybe I will."

She walked into the women's locker room to collect her things. She was glad to have the car tonight -- the forecast had predicted rain. Her roommates, the twins, Katelyn and Karyn, graciously gave her permission to use their car this evening, though she practically had to beg them to do so.

Katelyn Cross could be a wonderful friend but was real bitch as a roommate. In order to save money, Katelyn and her sister moved in with Bethany. For the most part, the three of them got along well enough, except when it came to the car. The twins hardly ever used it, yet they couldn't have been more possessive of the old vehicle. Any time Bethany asked to go to the mall or drive to class, an argument would break out. Even though she offered to pay for gas and upkeep, either one sister or the other would balk.

Boyce shut off the lights and locked up the office. He picked up his gym bag and waited by the front door for Bethany who was trotting from the locker room to the exit. He pulled out his cell phone and set it to mute.

"Hey, wanna go to Shannigan's and grab a beer? I'll buy."

"...so I told her that I was going to get it whether she liked it or not," Boyce said.

Bethany listened, still nursing her first beer.

It had been over an hour since she and Boyce first sat down at a corner table in Shannigan's. It was a spacious, Irish pub known in town for serving green beer on St. Patrick's Day and any other day that the owner felt like it. The college students loved the cheap prices and the locals loved the atmosphere. Strings of large paper shamrocks lined the walls and covered the ceiling. Maps of the old country graced the back of the bar as well as the bathroom stalls. Wooden plaques with quaint Irish sayings were plentiful.

Boyce was in his element. Tonight was his night. For once, he was free of that gnawing feeling in his gut, the one that reminded him of that damned shrew waiting at home with her chubby finger resting on speed dial. He was free from being nagged about coming home too late, free from any ugly confrontations. Margie and the kids were out of town until tomorrow evening.

Tonight there would be no boundaries.

"How long have you been married?"

"Too long," Boyce grumbled. "Actually, it's been about thirteen years, give or take a few months. I guess I'm one of those guys that don't keep track of dates or anniversaries."

"Oh, no. I bet your wife doesn't like that too much, huh?"

"Yeah, I guess not. Hey, why don't you let me get you a fresh beer? You've been playing with that one ever since we got here. It's got to be pretty warm and nasty by now."

"No, really, it's okay. I'm trying not to drink so much anyway. You know, empty carbs and all."

"Well, I'm going to have one more and then I'll drive you back to pick up your car, okay? Sound good?"

"Sure."

She excused herself and headed for the ladies' room. She wasn't used to drinking at all so one beer was enough to make her light-headed. She knew she needed to stay sober in order to drive home. She went into a stall, pulled her workout shorts down and squatted over the toilet. *It's so easy to pee after drinking alcohol.* The strong yellow stream eventually faded to droplets.

Bethany adjusted her clothes. She would have changed back into her shorts and shirt if she had the chance, but was caught off guard by Boyce's offer. She went to the sink to wash up. Her hair was a mess; stringy and still holding a tinge of perspiration. Her mind wandered into dangerous territory the longer she primped and fidgeted.

I can't believe I'm out with Boyce. I wonder if he can tell that I have a crush on him. Oh, my God, I would just die if he knew. I have to stay cool. I want him to like me back. Geez, Bethany – that is so stupid. He's married, you idiot. Maybe? No, no, come on. Be realistic. Maybe we can be friends. Maybe we already are? Why else would he ask me out? I never heard him ask any of the other girls out for a beer.

Bethany smiled and put her hand over her heart. It beat a little faster than before. When she looked into the mirror, she was blushing.

Boyce pulled into the gym's parking lot at exactly 11pm. Legally, he probably shouldn't have been behind the wheel, but no one was going to make demands on him tonight, lawful or otherwise. He unlocked the car doors and stepped outside, waiting for Bethany to exit the vehicle. She wasn't fall-down drunk, but the two beers she ended up drinking had put her into a mild funk. She slid out of the passenger's seat and stood. She blinked hard and rubbed her eyes. It took almost half a minute for her to register that the car was gone.

Katelyn's car was gone.

"What the hell? Where is it?" Bethany whirled around the empty parking lot. "What happened? *Where's the car?* Oh, my God. I locked it, I know I did. Remember? Before we left, I told you that I had to lock it up. I'm positive I did," she rambled.

"Hold on. Calm down, take it easy. Your roommate probably came out here and got the car because it was getting a little late, that's all. There's no reason to panic, okay?" Boyce said. He walked over and placed an arm around her shoulder.

"I - I just don't understand. What am I going to do? How could I lose a car? She'll kill me, I know it. You don't understand my room-mates and how bitchy they can be."

"Bethany, calm down. Let's go inside and figure it out together."

With no vehicle and no cell phone, she conceded to his offer. Boyce opened Slim Gym's door with his set of keys. She followed him into the entryway and waited by the office door. Boyce re-locked the front door behind him.

"Can I use the office phone real quick? It's a local number. I'll just be a minute."

"No."

"No, really," she smiled, "let me call them to see if they came and got the car. I promise it won't take long and then I'll call a cab. You probably want to get home yourself. Okay? Can you open the door?"

"No. No calls."

She cocked her head and looked at him incredulously.

"Come on, Boyce," she laughed out loud this time. "Stop kid-ding. I really need to see what happened. I need to know if they came and got it. I'll even walk home from here if you're in a hurry. Please just open the office door so I can call. I'll pay for it if that's what you're worried about."

"No, Bethany. No phone calls. Now, pick a locker room."

"*What?* I don't --"

"Pick. A. Locker. Room. Guys or girls. It's your choice."

"I...what are you talking about? Just open the office door."

Boyce approached Bethany -- his shadowy figure covered hers. The moonlight streaked in through the blinds, stabbing the situation with desperation and fear. She felt his arms wrap around her body and could smell the stench of cheap beer on his breath. He was perspiring now, one of those repulsive alcoholic sweats where naked skin feels chillingly moist and clammy to the touch. She tried to pull away, but that made him squeeze her harder against himself, against his growing virility.

"This is going to happen. Pick a room."

He whispered in her ear and made her heart race for a very different reason than before.

PERCHANCE TO DREAM

*J*ulie ran through the tall grass, spreading apart the overgrown weeds from her path. Biting thorns jabbed at her body. Sharp, bladed leaves angrily sliced into her bare legs, arms, and face. Within minutes, she was covered with scratches and cuts that would brand her skin for weeks to come.

Each step forward stirred up pollen and silt. She kept going until it became impossible to see through the hazy clouds of matter. She paused for a brief moment, trying to catch her breath, but even that was becoming a challenge. Every time she inhaled, granules of dust and tiny particles of fibers seeped into her nose and mouth. She coughed and hacked in a feeble attempt to keep her airway clear.

Her lips were parched. Her eyes blurred. Her skin was a like a tactical map laid bare for the elements to do their very worst. She turned her head, cocking it ever so slightly to the left, listening.

Heavy breathing. Trudging foot falls. He was not far behind.

She took off again, faster this time, fighting the wilderness that encompassed her. The sun pounded down with late summer fury as the cloudless sky held no relief in the way of rain.

Why can't he leave me alone?

She continued for what felt like hours. Finally, there was a break in the tall grass. The foliage opened itself up and led into a clearing.

A beach.

A beautiful, white sandy beach dotted with seashells -- where children's plastic pails and shovels were left near the water's edge. The ocean lapped at the shore in a rhythmic pattern, reaching further inland with each passing *wave. A lone seagull cried out; a jarring noise against an otherwise quiet moment.*

If she had been alone, she would spend time here; wading in the ocean, scouring the wet sand for snails, skipping tiny pebbles across the top of the water.

But she was not alone.

Her tennis shoes were wet now, heavy-laden with sand. Each step was becoming a chore, a weighted burden that slowed her progress. She stopped long enough to remove them from her feet, leaving them stranded on the empty beach for a hapless crab or some other creature to come upon and find a brief respite out of the sun.

Barefoot and exhausted, she pressed on, awkwardly padding her way across the sand. She thought that dumping her shoes would lessen her stilted gait and help her gain the speed she needed, but instead, the glass-like granules sucked her deeper in as she continued.

The shoreline was closing in around her feet and in the next moment, it was up to her calves. Straining and lunging, she threw her leg up, out, and over, stretching as far forward as her muscles and tendons would allow.

After gaining only a few more yards, she found the sand creeping upward, circling in around her knees. Panic set in; her breaths coming quicker now - shallow, staccato – making her lightheaded, causing more problems she did not need.

A few more steps.

Now the grit had settled around her thighs and was inching toward her waist. She clawed at the muck, flinging it into the air, digging and scraping like a dog, trying to free herself before the man got too close. She picked up a handful and pitched it to the right. That's when she saw him.

The man. The tall, blonde man wearing a light tan jacket, dark shorts, and a captain's hat.

He smiled at her.

She felt nauseous.

He took a step toward her and stopped, almost daring her to make the first move.

Without any rhyme or reason, she looked down at her feet and found herself standing on a clean sidewalk. Not taking the time to comprehend the incomprehensible, she began to run. She started off slowly, not fully certain, not quite trusting that the beige colored pavement was truly hard concrete and not merely a mirage made up of clumped sand.

Once her feet connected with the solid ground enough times to give her a sense of confidence, she picked up her pace until it became a full sprint.

She had no idea where she was headed, or even in what direction she should continue. The only thing that mattered was getting as far away from the man as she possibly could. If that meant running forever, then that's what she would do.

Why he was chasing her was the real question; a puzzle that had no answer. She didn't know him. She didn't want *to know him. In her gut and her mind and her soul, she knew he was the embodiment of evil. That was the only thing there was to know.*

She flew past house after house. Every single one had shuttered their blinds or closed their curtains. It was as if the people inside wanted no part of the devil they didn't know.

This was between her and the blonde man.

As she reached a crosswalk, she turned to look. Was he still behind her? If so, how far?

The man was strolling, STROLLING, up her side of the walk, whis-tling. He hadn't even broken a sweat. There wasn't a bead of sand on him, nor were his clothes the least bit ruffled. He looked as if he had just stepped out of a spa.

He eyed her.

She turned and began to run.

As she pumped her arms and gasped for breath, she wondered what would happen if he actually caught up to her. Somehow, in her heart, she knew the confrontation wouldn't involve rape or any other kind of physical assault. Surely it wasn't money he was after; she didn't have a cent on her person.

Then why fear him?

She didn't have the answer. She only knew that something horrible would happen if he ever caught her.

Block after block, mile after mile, she ran and he followed. How was it that all he had to do was walk casually, as if taking a leisurely Sunday stroll at the park, and yet she was expending every last bit of energy and willpower to stay ahead?

At last, she spotted a two-story house with an open door. Without a second thought, she ran from the sidewalk, up through the lawn, and pounded on the side of the screen door. For added measure, she pushed the doorbell and slammed her palm against the metal frame.

When no answer came, she glanced over her shoulder just in time to see the blonde man moving from the sidewalk and up onto the grass. He had stopped his tuneless whistling which made his sudden proximity much more threatening.

She reached for the handle and yanked it backwards. The door opened wide; the most welcoming vision she had seen in what felt like ages. Lunging forward, over the threshold and into the foyer, she saw a carpeted set of stairs in front of her. Taking two steps at a time, she bolted up, not even bothering to hold the handrail.

She spied a door leading out to the back of the house. Without a second to lose, she darted from the top of the stairs, through the kitchen, and slammed against the white painted door. She grasped the doorknob and turned it.

It was locked.

Fiddling with the knob, trying every conceivable variation, she couldn't unlock the door. It was at that moment that she heard him.

He laughed.

"I told you, Julie. You just don't remember. I will always be with you."

She squatted in the corner between the locked door and a kitchen cabinet, crouching down, curling up into a fetal ball like an abused child. She covered her face with her trembling hands, screaming 'no, no, no' over and over again.

When she opened her eyes, Julie was lying in bed, surrounded by three loving cats and a pile of blankets. The sun was beaming in, practically smiling on her and her furry friends. The yellow walls were covered with posters of her favorite bands and on the night-stand next to the bed was a pile of paperbacks; cozy mysteries and Victorian novels.

She wasn't wet or sweating or terrified. She was dressed in an old, worn tee-shirt and the most comfortable sweat pants she had ever felt. Each cat snuggled in close, soaking up her body heat and purring to their heart's content.

She rested her head back, sinking into the willowy down of the pillow and gently pulled the covers up around her shoulders. She took in a long, contemplative breath and let it out slowly, allowing her mind to drift into nothingness.

It felt like hours had passed before she felt the touch of feathery whiskers against her cheek, bringing her back into the consciousness of the morning. She giggled and reached up to pet her feline com-panion who was quietly purring in her ear.

When she opened her eyes, she was face to face with the blonde man who was crouched down next to her, smiling with a grin that was far too wide.

"Welcome back, Julie. You must have been dreaming. I hope it was about me."

AUCTION HOUSE

The small wooden gavel met the podium with a sound smack. Joe Snyder, lead auctioneer and one-third owner of the Princeton Antique Market House, pointed to a couple who were wearing matching Disney sweatshirts. This was their fifth winning bid today. These people had money and they weren't afraid to throw it around. Joe and his business partners, Bob Ritter and Warren Yount, would keep an eye on them.

The auction chant, or cattle rattle, as they referred to it, continued well into the late afternoon. They had three sizable lots to get through -- a long day by anyone's standards -- but the crowd had been receptive and compliant. By all respects, it was shaping up to be a lucrative auction for the men, something that they were counting on.

For the past six years, the Market House was a reliable source of income. Every auction brought in a full house. The past two summers, they actually had to open the side panels of the building in order to allow seating for all the bidders. Their reputation had steadily climbed and the men couldn't have been more proud.

But over the past few months, their sales had taken a hit. Buyers returned some of the merchandise, claiming there were problems with certain pieces, and requested their money back. Joe did *not* want to condone this practice, but Warren and Bob were adamant that they needed to put the customer first, even though all sales were supposed to be final. Exceptions *had* to be made for the good of the business. They agreed to bend their own rules, but it was done with the understanding that only 75% of the customer's money would be returned.

It was close to 5pm when the last item went up for bid and it didn't take long for the Disney couple to snag the final artifact. As people collected their belongings and filed out of the building, the Disney-clad man went outside to pull his truck around to the front door as his wife dug into her enormous patchwork quilt purse and fished out a macramé covered checkbook.

While Warren waited for the woman to complete her payment, Joe began stacking chairs. A few minutes earlier, Bob had disappeared into the back office to answer the phone. Just as the Disney-clad woman walked outside to join her husband, Bob let loose with a string of expletives.

"What's the problem?" Joe shouted in mid-lift, a wooden chair dangling precariously off of his index finger.

"Someone wants to return the acrylic; the one with the two ladies on the park bench."

"You're kidding me," Warren sighed. "What's *their* excuse for wanting to bring it back?"

"Well," Bob turned the corner from the office. "They were pretty vague at first and since it hasn't even been, what, *four hours* since they bought it, I asked if they would be willing to put it up in their house and live with it awhile. I mean, I can understand buyer's remorse, but *Jesus*."

"Yeah, I would have told them the same thing," Joe said.

"After I said that, they got really quiet, so I thought that was the end of it, you know? Finally, the guy said that they *had* to return it. They didn't even care about the money."

Joe and Warren looked at each other. After a very pregnant pause, Joe had to ask. "No refund? Alright, you got me. What's the catch?"

"No catch. These people were dead serious," Bob said. "They practically *begged* me to take it away."

"Why?"

"It scared them. The eyes in the painting scared them."

The streak of returns at the Market House seemed to grow over the next few months. The men could barely finish a day's auction without fielding calls from unhappy buyers pleading with them to take the paintings off of their hands.

The rule of all sales being final was completely thrown out the window. Joe and his partners were getting desperate, willing to try anything in order to keep their regular roster of bidders happy for future auctions. Word was beginning to spread like a thick layer of paste. If this downward spiral continued much longer, they would all be out of a job.

They met on a Sunday evening at Creamy's, the local pub just down the block from the auction house. They had a history of enjoying a pitcher or two after particularly profitable weekends at this watering hole where most of the employees knew them by name, by drink, or by their generous tips.

The staff at Creamy's was home grown; locals from the surrounding towns, including the day managers and the owner. One of the waitresses, Lana Howard, developed an instant crush on Joe from the first moment he walked into the bar a little over six years ago. It was on that first night when Joe, Warren, and Bob wrote up the initial business plan for the Market House -- in the corner booth right next to Ms. Pac Man. Since then, the men considered the place to be a second home and the workers like a second family.

Tonight's meeting, however, wasn't celebratory at all. An air of concern and desperation hung over them.

"Guys, how are we going to stop to these returns? Paintings have always been a major source of income for us. I don't know how we can exclude them when we're contracted to take everything else from the estates," Joe said. He gripped the handle of the chilled mug and swirled the last bit of beer. A thin coating of frost still coated the body of the glass.

"I agree with Joe," Warren said. He waved at Lana, held up three fingers, and pointed to their table. Without missing a beat, she nodded and went to the bar to round up more beer. "We can't afford to take partial pickups. We need to get to the bottom of it. Find out the real reason why these people are bringing stuff back. I mean, shit, some of these buyers are dropping a few grand *easy.*"

"Well, everyone that I've talked to has basically said the same thing," Joe added. "Something about the eyes scares them. When I asked if they could explain it, you know, give me more to go on, nobody had anything to add. Just came down to fear, pure and simple. It sure as hell wasn't about the money."

"That's pretty much what I've been hearing, too," Bob confirmed. "I've had people say that they're willing to forgo *any* kind of refund. They just wanted to be rid of the things."

As the men talked, Lana brought three full beer mugs and a large bowl of pretzels to the table. She grinned at Joe and blushed when he smiled and winked at her. Warren handed her a wrinkly twenty and told her to keep the change.

"Thanks, guys. I appreciate it. Let me know if you need anything else, 'kay?" Lana said. She turned and walked toward the bar with an exaggerated wiggle in her step.

"Someone still has a crush on you, man," Bob goaded Joe.

"Oh, knock it off," Joe shrugged. "She's a nice girl."

"Hey, that gives me an idea. Why don't we get an objective point of view on the situation? Let's ask Lana to take a look at the paintings we've got in the back. We won't mention that they've been returned. See if she notices anything out of the ordinary. If not, maybe the buyers are jacking us around. But, if she *does*, then why don't we bring in a fine art appraiser to do some in-depth research as to what the fuck is going on."

Warren and Joe nodded.

"Yeah, that could work. Good idea, Bob. Let's get an unbiased view on all this shit and stop hemorrhaging money."

Lana arrived at the Auction House the following evening wearing a green dress and white heels. She giggled when she walked through the door and saw Joe sitting at the counter by himself. Last night, when he initially asked her to come over, she thought it would be a quiet, intimate evening between the two of them. She imagined a picnic dinner, a sweet bouquet of flowers adorning the table, and just the right amount of candlelight. But as he continued to explain what he and his partners were after, her hope for a romantic-tinged night deflated. Still, they were friends. And helping each other out is what friends do.

"Thanks for coming over, Lana, we really appreciate it."

"It's not a problem, Joe. Anytime you need me, just ask."

Bob clapped his hands together. It was loud and jarring enough for Joe to shoot him a look. "Okay, then," Bob said, disregarding his partner's displeasure. He didn't want to waste time with idle chit chat. That's what Creamy's was for. "Lana, everything is ready for you in the back store room. All the paintings are lined up on the floor against the tables so you shouldn't have any problem seeing them clearly. Take your time. Really study each one. When you're done, come out here and let us know which one you like the best."

"I'm not in the market to buy anything, you guys. I thought you understood that when you told me about this yesterday."

"Wait, wait," Joe jumped in. "We don't want you to buy anything. Honest. It's just like I explained. We really want your opinion, okay? Please, will you do it for me?"

She smiled and walked over to Joe. He whispered something to her, making her laugh. She glanced at Warren and Bob while Joe continued to fill her ear with hushed words.

"Lana?" Bob asked. He held out his hand in a friendly gesture. "I'll be glad to look at your stuff."

"Great. Here, I'll show you where everything is."

Bob motioned her toward the store room. She followed obediently, high heels clicking loudly against the grey tiled floor, echoing off the walls. Before she disappeared through the doorway, she looked over her shoulder at Joe and gave him the tiniest wave.

After Lana was all set, Bob walked back to the front of the building and joined the other men. "Alright, guys," he said. "Now we just sit tight and wait. I don't imagine this'll take too long."

"How much do you want to bet that Lana doesn't see a thing wrong with any of those paintings," Joe said, eyeing the hallway. "You know, I'm starting to get the feeling that all of this shit is really about someone undercutting us. That our buyers actually found a better deal on eBay or another auction site."

"That's a bunch of bullshit, Joe," Warren said. "With all the research we do? All the connections we have? Nobody's undercutting us. If the people who bid on our stuff found any deals on the internet, they *might* be able to save like, five, ten dollars *at best*. No, it's gotta be something else."

A sudden pitch of shattering glass, snapping wood, and Lana's screams roared down the hallway. Pausing for only a second, Joe, Warren, and Bob bolted toward the back room. They found her on the ground - a quivering mass of sobbing flesh.

"Lana, *what happened*?" Joe pressed. He crouched down next to her, placing his hands on her trembling shoulders. Her bloodied hands covered her face as she rocked back and forth, mumbling and crying at the same time.

Bob and Warren looked around the store room at the fallen artifacts and broken merchandise. From what they could see, she had been alone the whole time.

"What happened back here? Did something fall on you? Are you hurt?"

Lana got to her feet with Joe's guidance, but she still guarded her face with her hands. She clumsily positioned herself in front of a painting which featured a man and a woman sitting next to one another on a bench. They were holding hands.

The lady was dressed in a Victorian-styled outfit, complete with a high neckline, full bell-shaped skirt, and a modest straw hat. The man looked just as dapper in his tweet sack coat and derby. With his free hand, he held a black walking stick. The scene behind them was just as pleasant; a spring afternoon with just a whisper of white clouds above them. In the far distance, children played with kites and chased wooden hoops near a babbling brook.

Joe looked at Lana and back again at the picture. He just couldn't put the two things together.

But Bob could.

"Holy shit!"

"What! What?" Joe and Warren shouted simultaneously.

"The eyes. The woman's eyes in the picture. *They're bleeding...*"

"That's because they're mine! She took them!" Lana shrieked.

She dropped her hands to her sides and raised her head toward the men. Her bloody eye sockets were empty. The men stood frozen, mouths agape, watching Lana claw at the air toward the painting.

"Give it to me!" Lana screamed. *"Give me that fuckin' picture so I can kill her and get my eyes back!"*

With one hand, Joe held Lana to keep her from stumbling into the painting, while he held his other hand over his mouth to keep from retching. The Victorian woman raised a monogrammed handkerchief up to her *new* eyes in order to wipe away a few drops of blood. Satisfied with her efforts, she tucked the cloth into her sleeve and the painting became a still life again.

Joe, Warren, and Bob looked at each other in disbelief. Each man silently questioned their own sanity at that moment.

"Joe, help me! Give me that goddamn thing so I can rip that bitch's face off!"

Joe didn't know what to say. All he could think to do was to hold her in a tight embrace.

"Those bastards came out of the painting! Don't you believe me?"

"Joe, behind you!" Bob shouted, pointing to a different picture sitting less than two feet from them.

This canvas was slightly larger than the one with the Victorian couple. It was a reproduction of an original Rembrandt, painted in muted golds with bronze overtones. The self-portrait of the artist was depicted as a partially shrouded figure who leered out toward an unseen audience.

The painter had become animated and was reaching for Joe's leg. Bob's warning came seconds too late. The skulking man had procured Joe's left ankle with one gnarled hand and amputated part of Joe's foot with a small scythe he held in the other hand. Joe shouted, let go of Lana, and reached toward his injured foot. Lana fell backwards into Bob's arms.

"This is insane. This is all fucking insane," Warren screamed. "We have to get Lana and Joe to a hospital right now and then go to police."

"Police? What the hell, man? What do you think they're gonna do? *These are fucking canvas!"* Bob shouted.

Warren was ready to argue Bob's point when he saw people in other paintings begin to move. It was almost undetectable at first. The motions were slow and subtle, but there *was* movement. The longer he looked, the more animated they became. Hands broke through the second dimension and reached into the third. Ghostly figures holding instruments of death began to climb over the frames and into the real world. Bob screamed.

Warren grabbed Joe by his collar and hoisted him up onto his good foot. He put his arm around his shoulder to stabilize his friend and headed for the front door.

"Joe, buddy, stay with me. We're going to the hospital right now, okay? Bob, bring Lana and let's go!"

In one quick motion, Bob scooped her up and ran after Warren. Once the four of them made it to Bob's truck, he gunned the engine and sped toward the nearest hospital which was fifteen miles away.

The picture frames in the back room were now empty. The people who were once in them were gone. And in all the chaos, no one thought to lock the auction house door.

WHEN THE EARTH BLED

M y name is Hallison Fischer and the first time I bent over to cut a swath in the earth, it bled. I'd never seen that before; a crimson line bubbling up from the grey dust that covered the ground. I suppose I never had the *need* to see such things since I hadn't been in the position to grow anything before. I was fortunate to have had a caring spouse, and before that, a father who would tend to such ghoulish work. They protected me from having to dirty my hands, and more so, *my eyes*, from such labors.

Over the years, I heard tales, snippets of gossip, and pieces of conversations - what it was like before the earth ran red with blood when it was cut open by sharp implements. Apparently, there were layers of dirt, or mud, sometimes clay. Occasionally, upon digging in the ground, a person might come upon a coin or hidden treasure buried by a child during their youthful innocence -- games such as "pirates" and the stowing away of prized trinkets from prying and curious adult eyes.

I tried to imagine what that must have been like -- to feel the dirt, to run barefoot over the soil and not have to worry about accidentally stepping into a gaping wound, a festering boil hidden among the sparse grasses which now covered the world. How incredible it must have felt to walk with abandon, or to run, throwing caution to the wind. To sit outside without a care in the world.

But all of those scenarios were not a part of my world. I had only seen such incredulous images in some of the few all-but-forgotten picture books scattered about. There was a smattering of them in the abandoned schools, and if you were careful and somewhat lucky, you might find one in a dinged-up old rusty locker.

Everything coincided around the time when the vaccinations stopped working and all the antibiotics had lost their effectiveness. People started dying. Thousands dropped so quickly, the morgues and crematoriums were overrun in a matter of weeks. The cemeteries filled up so fast, the local governments began asking anyone who owned any land, regardless of the size, to volunteer it, just to keep the bodies from piling up in the streets.

I remember when my parents signed up to help bury the dead. I had just turned sixteen. I thought about offering to help them, since the schools were closed by that point. What else could I do? Half of my friends were either dead or in the final throes of dying, while the others had been whisked away to 'safer parts of the country' by well-meaning but naive family members. Like there were any real safe parts left. Emails and texts connected us for a few months, until even the most basic technology proved unreliable. When you sent a message on Monday and received a *'cannot find recipient'* answer on Friday, you just sort of gave up.

It was my mom who put her foot down first, telling me that the job of burying bodies in mass graves was no task for a teenager, especially a girl. This was, of course, after I weakly offered, mostly from guilt. She said that she would rather have me stay home and read the few books they had squirreled away in order to soak up every bit of information that I possibly could. Such knowledge, she told me, might be useful in the future. I didn't give her much of an argument. I admit, I really didn't want to handle the corpses of our neighbors, but I thought that I should make the offer. I was, after all, their only child and didn't want to come across as lazy or uncaring.

My dad was a history buff and owned a few good books which described the specifics of World War III. He also subscribed to an underground magazine that still made handwritten printed issues. *Defying the Impossible* initially came out monthly, but trickled down to about every six weeks. I haven't seen a current issue for almost three and a half months now.

It was a fantastical rag, full of stories about people facing insurmountable situations yet enduring and overcoming the odds. As far as I knew, the articles were true; things that actually happened to people who survived long enough to tell their tales. I suppose they could have made stuff up, but I didn't want to believe that. The stories were inspiring. They spoke of hope and determination and an iron will, traits that we needed. Traits that were few and far between these days.

One issue in particular had the most amazing piece in it. The event took place over a hundred years ago, sometime in the 1940s. A doctor named Walter Freeman used to perform lobotomies by thrusting instruments similar to ice picks right above patients' eyes. He would move the tools back and forth in order to scramble the front part of the person's brain. There were times when he worked on two people simultaneously! While some patients suffered horrific results, others were supposedly made better, going on to live normal lives.

I couldn't believe it. If these people could live through such an atrocity, something so destructive and yet turn out okay, *even better* in some cases, then perhaps *my* family might just make it. The problem was that while no one was sticking metal rods above our eyes and swishing them around, we were dealing with our own kinds of monsters. The kind that decomposed from the inside out and fell dead at your feet as you sat across from them.

That was the scary thing; not knowing when death would snatch someone from the earth. I was too young to understand the details, but I remember my mom and dad talking about how all the medication in the world stopped working. After decades of being dependent on the drugs for one disease or another, people had simply become immune. Soon after, mutations of germs and viruses began wiping out populations on every continent.

When our town's population dropped from 3,000 to 1,000, the National Guard was called in, but they didn't last very long themselves. Within a year, we dropped to around 200. The schools closed, the malls and shops were shuttered, mail stopped being delivered, and all the grocery stores were looted. That's when we tried to grow our own food.

I don't know what happened to all the animals. After the end of World War III, there weren't many left – at least that's what we had been told in school. And who were we to question such things? I suppose it would be like people from the 1500s wondering where all the dinosaurs went. It just wasn't something most people thought about.

My dad, who had never planted a seed in his life, took to the soil, searching through our garage for tools, using rakes and snow shovels to create a garden of sorts. At first, he tried using seeds that my mom and I dug out of moldy apples and shriveled oranges. We let a few potatoes grow *eyes*. My dad said that once tubers had nubs or *eyes*, he could plant them and they would propagate into more potatoes – something he read in one of his books.

We did okay with the potatoes for a little while, but after the first year, nothing came up. Soon, we found ourselves heating bouillon cubes with lukewarm water and gathering the last bits of stale cereal the bottoms of boxes. We were trying to save special solid items, like hard candies and an old jar of green olives for a *real emergency*. Those didn't last long.

My mom went first. It was right after she buried a deformed baby on the hill next to my old school. I wasn't supposed to hear about it, but I did. I used to sit on the steps against the wall on the other side of the kitchen, listening to my parents talk about the horrific things they had seen during the day. How the gloves and masks ran out, how the skins from the bloated bodies would peel right off in their hands as they hoisted the dead from the back of pickup trucks and into the mass graves.

But it was the little baby that must have done my mom in. I heard her tell my dad how she tried to hold it carefully so as not to let any fluids touch her own scarred and scaly skin (from lack of nutrition). But she was tired and weak and hungry and in a moment of delirium, the baby's head rocked forward and slammed into her face. That was all it took. Its head popped like a distended pustule and my mom passed away within the week.

After that, my dad pretty much gave up. I couldn't blame him. He stopped volunteering and sat in his rocker day after day, staring blankly out the window. When I would bring him some tepid water flavored with an old beef bouillon cube, what I called *dinner*, he would stop rocking and make an attempt to smile at me. The day he stopped accepting my pitiful meals was the same day I became an orphan. I don't know – *can you be an orphan at sixteen?*

There was a college kid that lived down the street from us. It's funny. I say college kid, but the universities had been closed for years at that point. Still, I guess I'll always think of someone in their early twenties as a college kid. That's the way it should be, shouldn't it? Anyway, I only knew that his name was Ethan and that he was still around because he shouted hello and introduced himself one day while I was sitting on my stoop reading one of my dad's books last year.

The day after my dad passed, I walked down the block to see if Ethan would help me. It's not that I didn't want to bury my dad by myself, because, if truth be told, I would have preferred it. I didn't want to share my grief with anyone, especially with someone I didn't know. But physically, I needed the help and I hadn't seen any other able-bodied neighbors in quite some time. It wasn't as if I could get in the car and drive somewhere – there was no gas. I hadn't seen a working car in over seven months.

When I knocked on his door, it took two full minutes for him to answer. I mention this because I had seen him before as a strong, good-looking young man. But when he came to the door and I saw him up close for the first time, my heart as well as my expectations sank to the pit of my stomach.

He looked like an old man. His hair was shadowy wisps of its former self and his eyes were sunken and dark. What must have once been a youthful complexion was now as pallid and translucent as cellophane. He clung to the door jamb, his stooped posture still rather imposing at 6'2, and asked what he could do for me.

"It's my dad," I said.

Ethan nodded. Those days, you didn't need to say much more.

Silently, we walked back to my house. I let him in the back door and showed him where my dad was, still in the rocker, still with a blank expression. Together, we carried him out to the backyard and placed him gently on the patio. Ethan made a gesture that implied I should go back inside the house, that he would handle it from there. Without question, I obeyed.

From that point on, Ethan stayed with me at my house. We didn't talk much – what was there to really say – but it was good to have a companion. He helped me cut up my parents' leather shoes into strips and came up with the idea for ketchup soup from a bottle he had at his place. It was about three days after he first came over that we made the decision to get married.

It wasn't a real marriage; not in the legal sense. But we liked the idea of having an *'official'* bond between us. So, one evening as we were scraping together crumbs from the bottom of the toaster, Ethan took my hand and led me to the living room. We faced each other in front of the picture window and each made a declaration about sharing and helping and trusting the other person. I told him that I considered him to be my husband, and that if he wanted to, he could consider me his wife. He smiled and kissed me on top of my head, which only had the thinnest streaks of stringy hair left. Most of my scalp was scabbed over by then from all the scratching.

Lice – another thing we shared.

It's difficult to say exactly how long we were together. I would guess that Ethan lived at my house for another three days or so. Having only scraps to eat and questionably clean water to drink, I was surprised that we were able to stay afloat even that long. On the morning that he began coughing up blood, he told me that he was going into town for any supplies that might have been overlooked from past lootings.

I knew he was lying, but I didn't say anything. Even in our short time together, I realized that he was considerate enough to leave so I wouldn't have to bury a dead body all by myself. Plus, there were no supplies left at this point – those were long gone months ago.

Right before he left, we hugged each other and he leaned down to kiss me – not out of passion, but out of empathy. Two human beings shared a hellacious experience and were now parting company. A gesture of goodwill had to be offered.

I held up a hand as he walked out the front door and down the block. I stood there, smiling and waving until he rounded the corner and I couldn't see him anymore. I can't say for certain what happened to him, my husband of four or five days, but I still thank him in my mind for the acts of kindness he showed me.

He left four days ago. Since then, I finished the last of the ketchup and worked my way through the remnants of an old salad dressing bottle I fished out from a garbage can from the next block over. I ate a spoonful of parsley flakes for dinner last night with the laundry capful of water I siphoned out of the garden hose. It came out more *rust* than *water*, but there was still somewhat of a liquid quality to it.

Which brings me to today, when I cut my first bloody swath into the ground.

I didn't want anyone reading this letter, if there is anyone left to find it, to think that I was insane for doing what I was about to do. You see, there was nothing left to plant; no dried up seeds, no withered vines, no potato eye.

But I *was* harvesting. I cut into the dead world. I sliced open the top layer of dusty skin in order to reap what I could. Just beneath my feet, bodies were ripe for the picking. In most cases, *very ripe*. As

I penetrated the surface with my dull kitchen knife, a sickening primordial-like fluid oozed out from the slit. I kept hacking away until I saw the decomposing bodies that would keep my belly full. The earth was bleeding and I lapped it up like a dog.

SLEEP OVER

"Terry, which way do you sleep?"

"Huh?"

"Which way? Like, on your back or side or do you sleep on your stomach?" Suzanne asked. She glanced over at Terry as she placed her Partridge Family sleeping bag down against the far wall.

"God, I would never sleep on my stomach," Allison said.

Allison had already set up her belongings as close to the television as physically possible and was currently elbow-deep in a large bag of Fritos. Living next door to Kris, the birthday girl, gave her an edge on all the others. Not only did she get to arrive before anyone else, but she was able to stake her claim on what she believed was the best sleeping spot. As the Fritos disappeared into her mouth, Allison watched the other girls vie for positions on the shag carpet.

"Why not? What's wrong with sleeping face down?" Terry asked.

"Because then the guy can stab you in the back while you're sleeping," Suzanne and Kris answered, almost in unison. They looked at each other from across the family room and nodded in solidarity.

"Yeah, I heard that too. But you know what's worse? Lying on your side, 'cause then he can stab you from the front *and* the back," Brenda added.

"No, you wanna know the *worst* way you can sleep? On your back, 'cause then they can stab you right in the gut. That's where all your important organs are."

"This is stupid, you guys," Terry said. "Why are we talking about this? Nobody's gonna do anything like that with Kris's parents upstairs and all of us together down here. That stuff isn't scary anyway. I have four older brothers."

"Oh, my gosh, you guys! That's what we have to do later. We have to tell ghost stories!" Allison shouted.

All five girls squealed. They stood in the middle of the family room, jumping up and down, waving their hands in the air, and missing most of their attempts to high-five one another.

"And we have to raid the fridge!"

"And play Truth or Dare!"

"I can make fortune tellers!"

"And we have to play ghost in the graveyard! That's the best game in the world!"

"I don't want to go outside, you guys," Brenda whined. "It's too cold."

Allison and Kris rolled their eyes, both letting out a frustrated sigh.

"No, it's okay, Brenda. We'll just do stuff inside the house," Kris said. "Anyway, my parents promised that they'd stay upstairs all night. They won't come down here and bug us or anything. Well, my mom might come down later when the pizza gets here, but that's it."

"Do you have a Magic Eight Ball?" Terry asked, reaching for a can of Pringles.

"Yeah, it's up in my room. I'll go get it."

Kris ran up the stairs to her bedroom. Immediately, the four other girls closed ranks and began whispering about the presents they had brought and who among them could tell the scariest story.

"Okay, here it is," Kris said, bounding down the stairs a few minutes later. "My mom said the pizza should be here around eight-thirty. She ordered from that new place near the school."

"Here, give it. Let me go first," Suzanne said.

She shook the black eight ball as they sat in an egg-shaped formation in the middle of the family room. Allison brought along a few bowls of chips. Terry popped the top off of a chilled can of Fresca.

"Okay. My question is 'Will I be the first one to die in this group?'"
She turned the ball over to reveal her fate. It read: *Ask Again Later.*

The group laughed and made wide-eyed faces at each other.
Terry took the ball next.

"Okay, I have a question. My question is 'Am I going to be the
first person in our group to have sex?'"

"Terry, oh my God," Brenda gasped. "You can't ask that."

Allison shot Kris a look that could have turned into an eye roll,
but Kris looked away too soon. Terry shook the ball and turned it
over in her hands.

Outlook not so good.

"Okay, my turn," Kris stated as she held out her hands. "Ball, it's
my birthday so you have to give me a good answer."

"Hey, that's not fair. You can't tell it what to do."

"God, Brenda, it's a ball. It's not like it can hear her," Suzanne
snapped.

"Guys..."

"Okay. My question is 'Is this birthday going to be the best one
ever?'"

She shook it as hard as she could, turned it over, and held it out
so they could all read the floating answer.

Don't count on it.

The doorbell rang at precisely 8:30pm. The girls heard Mrs.
Roberts' footsteps descending the stairs, followed by the squealing of
the front door hinges. They listened as she chatted with the delivery
driver.

"Alright, the pizza's here. I am starving," Allison said. She placed
the empty Frito bag on a side table and rubbed her hands together.
"Do you have any other pop besides this stuff in the cooler?"

"Yeah, I'll get it. My mom keeps the Shasta Root Beer in the pantry. She doesn't know that *I know* it's there. She thinks she's hiding it behind the crock pot," Kris giggled and headed upstairs again.

"Girls, the pizzas are here," Mrs. Roberts announced.

She passed her daughter on the stairway as she carried three large cardboard boxes to the family room. On the top of the boxes, a cartoon of dancing, gooey pizza slices pointed to the phone number of Bazoni's Pizzeria. A thought bubble over one of the slices read '*mmmm, tasty*'.

The four girls swarmed in, taking the pizzas and thanking her for all the food.

"Have a good time, kids, and don't stay up too late."

"We won't, Mrs. Roberts," Brenda smirked. "I'll make sure that everyone's in bed by midnight." Mrs. Roberts smiled and headed upstairs. Suzanne threw a pillow at Brenda's head. It bounced off and landed near the closet door.

"Hey, quit it, you guys," Brenda yelped.

"Don't be such a brown nose. *We won't, Mrs. Roberts, I'll make sure they're in bed by midnight, Mrs. Roberts,*" Suzanne said, imitating Brenda's whiney voice almost to perfection.

This sent the other girls into fits of laughter seconds before an impromptu pillow fight broke out. When Kris returned with a paper bag full of pop cans, she dropped it on the floor and joined in immediately.

"Is this the bathroom?" Terry asked, pulling on a door knob.

"No," Kris answered, "that's our storage closet. The bathroom's around the corner from the laundry room over there."

"Okay, thanks."

"What's in there? Anything we can play with?" Allison asked.

"No, not really. It's just stuff like the vacuum, and suitcases, and extra chairs. It's always locked anyway 'cause that's where my mom hides her good jewelry, just in case there's a break in or something."

"I brought the Partridge Family game. We can play that," Suzanne offered.

"What about Life? I play that with my brothers all the time," Terry said.

"I think we should turn the lights off and tell ghost stories. I'll go first 'cause I have a really, really good one."

"Yeah, you guys. Let's do that."

The girls changed into pajamas, sped through a haphazard version of teeth brushing, and dragged their sleeping bags into the center of the room. The twelve-year-olds were oblivious to the chaotic disaster they were leaving in their wake. Bowls of half eaten chips, popcorn, and pop cans were strewn about the room. Empty paper plates that once held birthday cake had been precariously piled on top of one another on two of the end tables. Spoons, heavy-laden with goop and frosting had been wedged into a bowl of decorative plastic fruit. Wrapping paper overflowed from the lone garbage can. Bows and ribbons had been stuck on the closet door in the shape of a distorted smiley face.

At 11pm, the birthday girl demanded they shut the lights off. She wanted to hear Allison's stories. Once the whispers and giggles died down, she began. Suddenly, every creak and groan in the house became part of the story's backdrop. They huddled together, holding their pillows to their chests like shields to ward off any approaching horrors.

"...and then as they were walking up the creaky stairs, they heard..." Allison whispered. The other girls had to lean into the circle to hear her.

"I'm getting too scared, you guys. I think we should stop for a while and do something else," Brenda whined.

"Are you kidding? Why do you have to be such a baby?" Suzanne snapped.

"Shut up, guys. Let Allison finish her story," Kris said.

"Hey, did you just hear that?" Terry asked.

"Hear what?"

"Wait... there! That noise. I heard it a couple times," Terry said. She looked up at the ceiling as if she could see through to the second floor of the house.

"Yeah, I did. See, I told you that we should stop, but you thought I was being a baby," Brenda said. "It sounded like it came from the closet."

"No, the closet's locked. I already told you that. My parents keep a bunch of stuff in there and they have the only key."

"Are your mom and dad still up? Maybe it was them."

"I swear, you guys, I know it came from in there," Brenda insisted. She pointed to the door of the closet; the smiley face grinned, challenging her to see what was inside. Allison was more than a little miffed by the interruption. She couldn't help but blurt out her frustration.

"Well, go over there and open it if you're so sure there's something in there. Then I can finish the rest of my story."

"I'm not going way over there. *You* go."

"You guys are such a bunch of scaredy cats. It's a stupid closet. Just go and do it already," Terry said.

"*You* do it. You're the one with four brothers. You think that makes you so tough."

"Fine, I don't care. I'm not scared of a stupid door."

Terry stood and looked toward the rest of the group. It was too dark to see their expressions, but she could sense their apprehension. She hesitated for a moment, waiting to see if anyone else might join her, but no one volunteered. The idea of turning the lights back on *did* cross her mind, but she refused to show any vulnerability. She had represented herself as brave and tough throughout the entire evening, and she couldn't let that image waver now.

Terry stepped cautiously over the sleeping bags until her bare feet hit the linoleum. Someone whispered *hurry up.* She waved them off, but it was too dark for anyone to have seen the gesture. She tip-toed forward. Suzanne giggled.

"Shhh, you guys. Be quiet," Kris whispered and stifled a squeal of excitement into her pillow.

Terry inched closer to the door and reached for the knob. It was cold. One by one, her fingers gripped the brass ball. She turned it and pulled. Brenda screamed.

"Shut up," Terry hissed. "It's locked anyway. See?"

She tried twisting the handle to the left and right and then yanked on the knob for good measure. She kicked at the door, knocking one of the bows off in the process. The smiley face was now missing an eye.

"What was the noise then? Where'd it come from?" Kris asked.

"Can I just go back to my story? I was getting to the good part."

"Yeah, go ahead," Kris said, turning her back on Terry and the closet door.

A gurgling noise floated over the family room. It sounded different than the one before, but it was louder and most certainly closer. Terry ran over to join the rest of the girls. They held on tightly to each other.

"Oh, my God, what *is* that? Kris, go upstairs and see if that's your parents. Then come back down and tell us what it was."

"No way," she protested. "If I go up there *now*, my mom will make us go to bed. They'll be mad, 'cause they're probably asleep already. They go to bed early."

"C'mon, please? Just go up there. Pretend you're getting something out of your bedroom."

"No. I'm not gonna..." Kris started to answer but stopped when everyone heard the sound again.

"That was really close, you guys. Seriously, I think we should get your parents, Kris."

"You're always serious, Brenda," Suzanne sighed. "You know what it is? It's probably just a tree branch hitting a window or something. Everybody's making a big deal about something stupid."

"A tree branch hitting a window from *inside* the house?" Terry asked. She was glaring at Suzanne. *"That* sounds pretty stupid if you ask me. Maybe we all *should* go upstairs."

"I'm not going up there and I'm not waking Kris's parents either."

"C'mon, Brenda. This is *my* house. You know my house - there's nothing scary about it. You've all been here before. You've slept over tons of times. You weren't scared then."

"Well, if it's not scary, then *you* go get your parents and we'll wait down here," Suzanne snipped. Out of all her friends, Kris liked Suzanne the least.

"I'll go with you, Kris. I'm not a *baby* like Suzanne is," Terry offered. She stuck her tongue out at Suzanne who reciprocated back immediately. Kris was already on the third step by the time Terry joined her.

"Do you think we should go with them?" Brenda whispered to Suzanne and Allison, hoping they would say no.

"You can go if you're so worried. And if no one is telling ghost stories anymore, I'm going to sleep. I'm tired and this is getting boring," Suzanne mumbled. She crawled into her sleeping bag and flipped her pillow over so she could lay her head directly on top of David Cassidy's face.

"Yeah, if Kris' parents come down here, I don't want them yelling at us or anything. If we look like we're sleeping, at least *we* won't get in trouble," Allison said. She took a giant swig of Coke and set it on the floor next to her head.

The entire second floor of the house was dark and tucked in for the night. Terry blindly followed Kris down the carpeted hallway, both girls tip-toeing and shushing each other as if they were prowlers trying to make an escape. They headed toward the bedroom which was on the left at the far end of the corridor. Mr. and Mrs. Roberts usually went to bed right after the ten o'clock news, so when the girls found their bedroom door shut, Kris didn't see it as anything out of the ordinary.

"Are you sure we should wake them up just 'cause we heard a noise? I'm starting to feel kind of bad about this, Kris."

"Well, I don't know..." she paused.

They stood outside the closed door, unsure of what their next move should be. Their furrowed brows and downturned mouths easily conveyed worry, but the hesitation in Terry's voice made her anxiety painfully obvious.

"You know, Allison *was* in the middle of telling a scary story and then everything just got kinda weird. C'mon, don't wake 'em. Let's just go back downstairs and find something else to do, okay?"

"Yeah, I guess you're right. I just thought that..." Kris started but paused the second both she and Terry heard a shrill gasp. It came from downstairs. The two frightened girls began banging against the bedroom door until it flew open. In a panic, they stumbled into the room.

"Mom! Mom! We heard something downstairs!"

"Please hurry," Terry added.

"Dad? Dad! Wake up, there's weird noises in the house!"

Kris turned on the lamp that sat atop her mom's nightstand. The small bulb cast an eerie glow, elongating shadows and stretching silhouettes like gangly tentacles reaching out to capture prey. The girls looked down at the king-sized bed. The shape of two bodies, made from pillows, blankets, and bed sheets, lay on either side of the bed in the spots where Kris's parents had once slept.

"Mom?"

"Where'd they go, Kris?"

"Mom! Dad?"

"Would they leave the house without telling you?"

"Mom, where are you?!"

"We better get everybody else. Then we'll go through the house together, okay?"

Kris nodded, letting Terry take the lead back down the hallway to the stairs and down to the family room. But before she crossed her parents' bedroom's threshold, Kris glanced back at the two piles of bedding. They looked a little too much like mounds on top of fresh graves for her liking.

They thundered down the two flights of stairs, taking two steps at a time when they could. Already out of breath and trembling, Kris and Terry ran over to the three who had apparently fallen asleep in their absence. They shook the sleeping bags, shouting over each girl's head.

"Allison, wake up. Kris's parents weren't there. We have to look for them!"

"Suzanne! Brenda! Hurry, get up! We need you guys!"

"Allison? *Allison?*"

"Kris," Terry yelled. "Go turn the lights on. Hurry!"

Kris ran to the switch and flipped it on.

Terry pulled the top part of Suzanne's Partridge Family sleeping bag down and then screamed. Suzanne lay on her left side. The angle made it easy for Terry to see a large chef's knife sticking out of Suzanne's chest while a smaller carving knife protruded from her back. The bag was soaked through with dark red blood, giving the Partridge Family's smiling faces a dark, macabre pallor. The warm liquid was already spreading away from the body, seeping over to the linoleum floor. Both knives had obviously been thrust in with a great deal of force; the only parts visible were the black handles. A thin line of blood trickled from the corner of Suzanne's mouth.

Kris shrieked. Terry threw the cover back over Suzanne and went over to Allison, who was face up, staring blankly at the ceiling. Kris shook her head violently, but Terry grabbed the top sheet and pulled it down. A serrated bread knife stuck straight up from Allison's chest like an exclamation point. A path of warm blood had already grown from the blade's point of contact on her body down toward the edge of her nightgown. Kris and Terry screamed again and started to cry. Terry turned toward Brenda's bag.

"Don't --" Kris pleaded.

Terry ignored the plea and eased the sleeping bag down. A huge meat cleaver jutted out from the middle of the girl's back.

Terry ran over to Kris. They continued to cry and scream as they clung to one another, frozen to the spot. *What were they supposed to do now?* In their shock and confusion, neither girl noticed that the closet door was now ajar and a thin, sickly, barely audible, off-key rendering of *"Happy Birthday"* was emerging from the darkness within.

33 1/3

Mark DeSoto opened the wildly stickered door to Doomed Head Records, a heavy metal music shop that had recently put a want ad in the local alternative paper. The ad asked interested applicants to have flexible hours available for scheduling purposes; no other requirements were listed. Mark had been looking for an entry level job in the music scene, so working in a store like this would not only be a great opportunity, but a way to gain some experience.

What especially caught his eye was the last phrase under the address: *If you have any of these bands on your iPod: Journey, Justin Bieber, Genesis, assorted boy bands, or anything that appears on an Adult Contemporary chart, let's end our relationship right now. Don't bother coming in.* He thought that showed real class – he understood these people already.

"Hello? Is anyone here?"

Mark peered into the store and looked around. The place seemed more like a loft apartment instead of a place of business. The layout had a funky vibe. There were a few steps leading up or heading down to record bins. CD towers and private listening areas were tucked away in nooks, complete with headphones, body pillows, and artist lists. Black and white linoleum tile covered the floor like an overgrown chess board. The walls and ceiling were decorated with music posters and handmade artifacts.

He recognized a number of the bands and was intrigued by the art surrounding them. Mark was used to the satanic emblems. Goat heads, pentagrams, and hellacious scenes were all part of the heavy metal music genre, but it was all fairly innocuous. The most important thing was the music, not necessarily the imagery that went with it.

"Hey, man, sorry to keep you waiting. We just got a shipment of new arrivals in the back. Are you here about the job or are you looking for some music?"

"The job. Yeah. And I brought my resume if that'll help."

"Cool. My name's Evan. I'm the owner here. Let me take that and I'll have you fill out an application. When you finish, just give a yell, okay?"

Mark took the papers from Evan and watched as he disappeared between the curtains. He took a seat at one of the listening areas and scrounged around the bottom of his backpack for a pen. As he bent down, he accidently knocked a tiny rubber goblin off the counter. *Cute*, he thought, *they have a sense of humor here.*

Halfway through filling out the paperwork, he stopped for a quick stretch. He couldn't count the number of times he had written the exact same information on every job application. Why couldn't he just talk about the music and to hell with trying to remember the address of his old elementary school?

He glanced around. There was so much to see. His eyes fell upon a vintage turntable. There was a record on it, but something was on top of the record. Mark spied the curtain that separated the store from the back room. He didn't want Evan popping out all of a sudden and find him messing around with anything. As quietly as he could, he stepped a little closer to the phonograph. His eyes grew wide and his mouth fell open.

In addition to the album, a human head rotated on the record player's spindle at the speed of 33 1/3.

As the days passed, Mark spent much of his free time lying on his bed, listening to old Metallica records with his eyes closed. He had filled out applications at every other music store in the city, but never received so much as a rejection letter. He was *really* counting on this one to come through. Delivering pizzas for minimum wage and receiving pathetic tips from college students was getting pretty old.

The one thing that bugged him the most about Doomed Head was that damn rotating cranium. No matter what he did in the days that followed, he couldn't get that image out of his mind. The thought of it chilled him and he wondered if he could work in a place with that thing staring at him all day.

"It couldn't have been real, dude," his longtime friend, Janis, re-assured him over the phone. "Stores like that always have a bunch of crazy shit all over the place. It's nothing, man. Look, if they offer you a job, take it and then get *me* hired on."

"I don't know, Jan. It looked pretty fuckin' real to me."

"How close were you to it?"

"I dunno. Like five feet or something. Maybe a little less."

"See, man? Everything looks fuckin' real from that far away. You've seen those special effects shows and how they do all that make-up shit on actors. That's all it is, dude. That's all it is."

That same evening, Janis stopped by Mark's apartment to share a few joints he had personally rolled earlier that afternoon. He knew Mark needed to relax and a bit of weed had always been the per-fect answer. The two friends smoked and talked well into the night, only breaking the conversation to walk down the block to White Castle where they ordered three dozen sliders and a few boxes of fries around 4am.

When Mark finally received his first paycheck from Doomed Head some three weeks later, he wanted to pin it up on his bulletin board rather than cash it. *This is really it,* he thought. *This is where my career in the music business begins.* He studied the blue security paper and ran his hands over the amount typed in blue ink.

What got him up at 10am every morning, however, wasn't the money. It was the fact that he was becoming part of the team at the shop. His co-workers didn't treat him like *the new guy.* When he came in Tuesday through Saturday at 11am for his eight hour shift, they were genuinely happy to see him. His previous jobs, including the pizza delivery one he had recently quit, had been tolerable at best and redundant as hell at their worst. Landing a gig at the record store with guys who were actually cool was a godsend. He *enjoyed* going to work these days.

Evan peeked out from behind the curtain that separated the two areas and shouted to Mark.

"Hey. We've gotta take care of some stuff in the back for a while. Could you watch the front and finish cleaning over near the new releases?"

"Sure, man, no problem."

He gave Evan a wave and went to grab a rag and the bottle of cleaner from under the counter. Mark watched Anthony and Harris, the two other employees, disappear behind the curtain as well, leaving him alone. It had been a slow afternoon, so he wasn't too worried about becoming overwhelmed with customers. That tended to happen later in the day.

He sprayed the bins and racks and wiped them down, methodically working his way over to the turntable. He had looked at it, studied it, and even touched it, but Janis was right. It *couldn't* be real. But there was still something unsettling about its complexion. The texture of its skin and the details of the face were downright haunting. For three weeks, he had dusted it, unpacked boxes around it, and leaned over it, yet nothing about the head changed. He didn't want to ask Evan or the other guys about it because he didn't want to come off looking like a pussy, or worse, *uncool.*

He squirted more cleaning fluid on the rag and ran it over the surrounding components. For a moment, he stopped to untangle a couple of wires on the floor. As he stood up, he came face to face with the head which now had its eyes open and its mouth wide in a silent scream.

"Holy *shit*!"

Evan appeared from the back room just in time to see Mark stumble backwards into a cardboard display of sale CDs. Cases and discs went flying.

"What the hell, Mark? What's going on?"

"That," he pointed, jabbing his finger toward the turntable. "That head opened its eyes and tried to scream. I am not shitting you, man. I saw it."

"Okay, I know. Sometimes she does that. It's just a reflex, you know, like when your eyelid starts spazzing because you're tired. She won't hurt you. Why don't you take a break from cleaning today, alright? How about alphabetizing those new bins of CDs instead?" Evan winked and chuckled at Mark before turning his attention to the back room. The curtains fluttered and in the next instant he was gone.

Mark staggered to his feet as he regained his composure. He was a little more than embarrassed, but wasn't really ready to let the whole situation go.

"Evan? *Evan?*" He called toward the swaying black curtain, but either Evan didn't hear him or chose *not* to.

He straightened up the mess he made and put the cleaning supplies away. After a quick glance at the door, confident that no customers were about to approach, Mark walked toward the back room. He wanted – no, *needed* – to understand what Evan meant by '*sometimes she just does that*'.

As he reached for the curtain, he heard Anthony raving about a new album that had come in with the latest shipment. Mark had never been allowed in the back room. Evan had made it very clear from day one that working in the back was by invitation only.

"If you learn the front of the house first, the back room stuff will be a breeze. When you're ready, I'll *know*. For now, leave it for Anthony and Harris."

But at *this* moment, after the bizarre conversation about the head, Mark needed clarification, which meant going through the curtain uninvited. He slipped through the opening and saw Evan, Anthony, and Harris gazing up at a beautifully colored vinyl record. Harris held it toward the ceiling light. The disc was a standard twelve inch, but the pattern was a *splatter*, which meant that assorted colors of vinyl were sprinkled onto a background before being pressed. This particular album was oozing and pulsating.

"Mark, what the hell are you doing back here? You need to be out front watching the store."

"I wanted to ask you about the head."

"I told you. Don't worry about it."

"Why is that record dripping?"

"Just pressed, Mark," Harris offered. "You want to see it up close? I'll bet you never held a record like this before."

Mark stepped toward the throbbing disc. Evan and Anthony stepped out of the way as Harris handed the album to Mark. They all wanted to hear their new associate's reaction to the experience.

"It's warm."

"Yeah, they usually are at first."

"And it's, I don't know, *leaking*? Why would it leak? I've never owned a record that dripped."

"Well, this is a special pressing," Harris began to explain. "Some pressing plants add dyed vinyl for color splatters, but we add…"

Evan cut him off before he could finish. "Harris, we don't need to go into all that now. I want Mark to get comfortable with the front of the store first. The three of us can handle the rest."

Mark glanced back and forth between the record and his boss.

"No, tell me. Just because I haven't been here as long as you guys doesn't mean I'm not as committed to the shop. I need to know our products just as well as you do. *It's all about the customers, right?*"

Harris smiled. He liked the fact that Mark was ready to be on board. While it was true that merchandise had been practically flying off the shelves over the past few months, it still took time to prepare it for the sales floor, and the more people involved the *better*. The faster a new employee picked up the entire business model – the back and front of the house - the more profit they *all* made.

With the extra money, they could start advertising to a wider audience through the internet. They could start shipping pieces. There were plans for opening a distribution center. Ideally, Evan, Harris, and Anthony wanted to open a second store in Chicago, or maybe Detroit. If Mark was this eager to learn after such a short time, Harris was certain nothing could stop Doomed Head from becoming a financial success.

"That particular record you're holding is from our Myrna collection," Harris said.

"I've never heard of that label. Is it new?"

"It's not a label, Mark. It's a person. Myrna was a fresh kill just a few days ago and her spleen was really amazing. That's what you're appreciating right now, buddy. It tasted like shit, so we used the rest of it in our pressing. Anthony does incredible artwork, doesn't he? You like to emphasize the spleen or lungs, don't you?"

"They're my favorites," he whispered, admiring his own work.

"Yeah. This was a good kill. Beautiful, isn't it?"

Mark stood with his mouth open, directing and redirecting his focus between the three men. He set the dripping record down carefully onto the covered workstation. An angry red ring soaked into the cloth and through to the wooden table below. It would leave a mark that wouldn't quite come out, regardless of how hard Evan would scrub it in the days to follow. They would need to buy a thicker pad.

Mark blinked slowly, cleared his throat, and spoke.

"You are not shitting, guys. That is indeed, *beautiful*."

Janis woke up early. He wanted to be out the door before the rest of the city came to life. He shot his boss at *We Got Your Back* a quick email, telling him that he couldn't come in that day, that something had suddenly come up.

He averaged about twenty-five hours a week at the mall, persuading senior citizens to purchase the extra soft cushions for their toilet seats. According to the brochure, *the elderly spend a great deal of time 'visiting the oval office', so why not make it a comfortable, inviting place to set a spell? Read, relax, and take a load off on the comfort of your own Commode Cushion.*

Janis hated the fact that he was required to tell his customers that they could 'ease the pushin' with a Commode Cushion'. That line alone should have driven him to look for another job. But he wanted to work in the *music* business, just like Mark. He didn't want another lame-ass job in retail to replace the one he already had.

Last week, Janis called him to see if he had put in a good word for him at Doomed Head. He was pretty hopeful since Mark had done nothing but rave about the place and say how cool everyone had been since he started. However, instead of giving him good news about possible employment, Mark ended up explaining the barbaric procedures he was being taught in order to make music-related artifacts for the store.

At first listen, Janis figured that his buddy must be pretty damned high to come up with the shit he was telling him. *Killing homeless people in order to use parts of their organs for record pressings? Crafting hair and skin into wall art? Occasionally ingesting pieces of human tissue, just because they liked the taste of it?* Surely Mark was having a bad trip on formaldehyde-laced weed in order to come up with maniacal stories like that.

But after they hung up, Janis thought back on something he had read in the paper. Homeless people had gone missing, especially ones that camped out near the old railroad yards on the city's west side. Some of the regulars at the local shelters had suddenly stopped coming in; a break in their routine that put the staff on alert.

He hadn't given it much thought before, but now the connection between the missing persons and Mark's accounts were a little more than coincidental. It was something about the way he described in graphic detail how Evan and Harris tracked down a potential kill, dismembered it, and preserved the pieces for their projects that was *beyond* unsettling. It bordered on ghoulish.

Janis initially planned to investigate before turning his friend in to the authorities. He didn't want to believe that murder, cannibalism, and worse yet, metal-heads participating in artistic creativity, were happening at the music shop. But the more he read about the missing homeless (what the police were calling 'the hobo killings') and the more he heard Mark's pontifications about the latest pieces for sale, he simply couldn't shake the horrific association between the two.

The 17th Precinct sat in the middle of the city amidst other governmental buildings, attorneys' offices, and a few coffee shops. It was located far enough away from Doomed Head Records that Janis felt comfortable to ride his bike down Main Street without continuously looking to see if Mark was in the vicinity.

With a heavy sense of trepidation, Janis pulled open the glass door of the police department and stood in the lobby. A uniformed officer came up from behind and placed a hand on his shoulder. Janis was startled and gulped in an extra serving of air, immediately setting off an embarrassing cacophony of hiccups.

"Son, can I help you with something? You look a little lost."

"Uh, (hic), yes, sir. I wanted to talk to somebody about the homeless (hic) killings."

"Why don't you come over here and have a seat at my desk, okay? But, let me get you some water for those hiccups so we can talk."

Janis placed his backpack on the ground in front of his feet and took a seat on the hard wooden chair. He covered his mouth in order to insulate the hiccups, but it only made him look spastic.

"Here you go," the officer said, handing him a Styrofoam cup of water. "And here's my card. I'm Officer Bronsky. Now, can I have your name?"

"Janis Dumont (hic)."

"Address and phone?"

"148 Euclid. 357-1982."

"Okay. You mentioned the homeless killings. What kind of information do you have?"

Janis started at the beginning, telling the officer about Doomed Head Records and how his friend had managed to score a job there. He admitted to being jealous but was hoping to land a position anyway. That was, until he heard about their insidious art pieces and record pressings. He repeated everything he could remember about the procedures, the splatter albums, and how the killings were scheduled in time for the new release of merchandise.

He thought he was making a pretty solid case, but before he had spit out the first sentence, Bronsky's gaze had dropped to Janis's green backpack; specifically to the emblems and patches touting the wonders of weed. At that point, the officer stopped taking notes and, as standard operating procedure dictated, let the citizen vent. After Janis finished his story, the policeman stood up.

"Alright, Mr. Dumont, I think I have everything I need. You have my card if there's anything else you would like to add. We appreciate you stopping by and sharing your information."

He escorted Janis to the exit and held up his hand in a friendly gesture as he left the building. Bronsky pulled the glass door shut and walked back to his desk, shaking his head.

"Delusional potheads. They come up with the craziest shit."

Janis realized that talking to the police was a dead end. He wasn't high and he wasn't stupid. It was screamingly obvious to him that Bronsky didn't take him seriously, especially after being abruptly escorted from the premises. But before he could figure out his next move, he needed to call Mark at the record store. He *had* to know, one way or the other, about the murders and his friend's possible involvement.

"Hey bud, what's up? You want to come over and hang out tonight?"

"Sorry, man. Harris and I are going on a materials run. *My first one.* I am so stoked. I think it'll be pretty late by the time we get back, so I gotta take a rain check. Next time though, okay?"

"Mark, just tell me. Are you really killing people? Are you cutting them up and making records? And *selling* them? Come on man, talk to me. Are you honest to God *eating human remains or are you just majorly fucking with me all this time?*"

"Ah...Janis," Mark choked out. "I-I'm not gonna get into this with you now. I need to get back to work. I'll call you later, okay?"

:click:

"Wait. Mark? Shit."

Janis pedaled for hours through the city, giving him time to formulate some sort of plan. Finally, he stopped off at a hardware store, gathering supplies that he would need to make this right. Snippets of discussions with his friend played over in his mind. *Like a broken record*, he thought. But something had to be done. *Someone had to stop this killing spree.* He waited until Doomed Head Records closed for the night to make his move.

It was just after 11pm when, from a nearby café, Janis watched as Evan shut off the lights, locked the main door to the shop, and walk to his car. Janis tossed a dollar bill on the table next to a partially empty coffee cup and stood. He hoisted his backpack from the booth and looped it over his right shoulder, leaving the place empty, except for a waitress dressed in a pink skirt and white top who was busy checking her phone.

Beside for a lone drunk staggering around the street at that hour, no one noticed as Janis Dumont navigated his bike around to the back of Doomed Head Records. Without hesitation, he took a gas can and a book of matches from his bag and proceeded to set fire to the store.

The next morning, he hitched a ride with a van heading to Missouri. As far as he was concerned, he was done, not only with Doomed Head Records but with Mark as well.

"Hey, Janis, it's Mark. You know I hate leaving fucking messages on your phone, dude, but I haven't heard from you in like, a week. Your boss said that you haven't been in to work, either. Are you sick, man? Well, hope you're okay. Just wanted to tell you…by now, you probably heard about the fire at the store. The thing is, even though we lost a bunch of shit - *cool shit* - Evan is getting a ton of insurance money. He's going to re-open *this* store, and still have enough money to open another one in Chicago. *There's tons of homeless there.* I put in a good word for you. But being the *new* guy, you'll have to learn the front of the store *first*, just like I did."

FREE WHEELERS

Charlie Edgebottom, the young, overly eager salesperson at Wheels and Deals, was practically drooling over the two men who had been examining the new bike racks. They had the distinct *look* and *sound* of serious buyers. He had been eavesdropping on their conversation for the better part of a quarter of an hour while he pretended to rearrange the decals on the counter carousel. He hadn't made a sale all afternoon and no matter what it took, he wasn't about to let these guys walk out the door empty-handed. The two men, however, were painfully aware of Charlie's presence but did their best to ignore the just-past-pubescent's mouth-breathing and longing stares.

Wheels and Deals was the lone bike shop in the small town of Crandle, population 3,233. The city of Lemont, population 18,088, which was home to three mid-level stores with a wider selection, was a good thirty-five miles away, and that was with the wind at your back.

Mark Bass and Kevin Wylie, best friends since grade school, had recently graduated from Iowa State University with degrees in Business Administration and Marketing, respectively. Both men shared similar qualities; tall, lean, blonde hair, and a love of biking. They were looking to score a small-town deal and not have to drive into the larger town.

Charlie couldn't contain himself any longer.

"The great thing about *these* bikes is the GPS system that comes with them. See, they're already attached to the crossbars. I know the price of the bike is probably a little higher than what you planned to pay, but these are very aerodynamic. These come with a two page list of features specific to this model. The older ones can't even begin to compare."

Mark looked down at the teenager. Charlie's glasses were askew and he actually had scotch tape wrapped around the center bridge. It was all Mark could do to stop himself from asking this guy if he played D&D on Sundays in his mom's basement.

"Well, I don't think that's the kind of bike we're after, but thanks anyway."

"What about these two over here in the corner?" Kevin asked.

Charlie looked uncomfortable. His face turned a whiter shade of pale, if that was humanly possible, and his upper lip began to tremble. He scuttled over to Kevin and picked up a tarp from the floor.

"I-I, uh, don't know how these got onto the sales floor. Um, these aren't really for sale. They shouldn't have been out here. I mean, you guys are obviously experienced riders. You're looking for quality machines that won't nickel and dime you to death."

Mark moved closer and began inspecting the bikes. Kevin straddled one and began testing the gears and gadgets.

"These are just the kind we were looking for. But, I don't see a price on 'em."

"Yeah," Kevin agreed, "These are *perfect,* actually. You don't mind if we try these out, do you? You know, take 'em for a spin outside? See how they handle?"

Charlie was beside himself. He looked back and forth, from Kevin to Mark and back again, sputtering something about how they should have never been on the floor and that they should wait to talk to the manager who would be back from vacation next Tuesday. The two men ignored him.

"Good idea," Mark said. "I don't mind the green one if you want to take the blue one, man. Either way works for me."

"Cool."

Charlie continued to try and dissuade them but it was obvious that all of his concerns and warnings were falling on deaf ears. With a sigh of resignation, the teen walked to the front of the store and held the doors open for the men. They hopped up onto their respective seats, peddled off the lot, and headed toward the park for a quick test drive.

"We'll take 'em," Mark said. He pulled his wallet out from his back pocket and turned to Kevin. "Let me put it on my card and you can pay me back later, okay?"

"Sounds good."

"Look. Guys. I can't sell these to you. They aren't for sale. Let me show you some sweet rides that came in just last weekend. You'll love 'em even more than these ones, I promise."

"We want *these* bikes, alright? I don't care about the cost. And we're not interested in any other 'sweet rides'. Just ring us up and we'll get out of your hair."

"Yeah, come on, man. What's the problem? Don't you want to make a sale today?" Kevin added.

"Guys, it's really not about that. I'm just..."

"Look, I worked a ton of retail during college. Everyone knows what a bitch working on commission can be. I worked at Maynard's selling dress shirts and ties to asshole businessmen who brought their nagging wives along and it totally sucked. All the guys ever wanted to do was to pick something out, *maybe* try it on and get the hell out of there. But the wife always, and I mean, *always* was like, 'try this one, dear,' or 'I don't like that pattern'. I'd have tons of clothes all over the place. You know, everything unpinned, hangers everywhere. Then, just like clockwork, the wife would say, 'let's go and see what the others stores have.' No matter how hard I tried, they would end up buying one pair of fucking socks. Retail plain sucks – we get it."

"That's really not what I meant. I'm not even sure what that story has to do with..." Charlie started but Mark cut him off in mid-sentence.

"If you're looking for a bigger commission, we're sorry. We're only interested in the bikes right now."

The teen shook his head and took out a sales slip. He wrote up the price of each bike at $399, hundreds less than the new 'sweet rides' and the rest of the inventory. Mark signed off on it and paperwork exchanged hands.

Charlie silently watched as the two men walked their new bikes out of Wheels and Deals, attached them to the back of their truck, and drove away. Once the vehicle was out of sight, Charlie ran to the bathroom and slapped himself in the face.

"You idiot. You should have put 'em in the back room when you were told."

Kevin and Mark were up at the crack of roosters the next morning. The Weather Channel confirmed a perfect day for riding; a slightly breezy 70 degrees with just a hint of cloud cover in the late afternoon. It was an opportunity they weren't about to squander.

Maps of biking trails marked in yellow highlighter were strewn about the dining room table. Backpacks filled with water, snacks, and first aid supplies waited near the front door. For good measure, Mark tossed a compass in his bag on the off chance their Smartphone GPS wouldn't pick up a signal.

The plan was to leave at nine and ride until about eleven. That would get them to Decker's Pond in time for lunch. From that point, they would head further north for another few hours, turn around, and make it home by six, seven at the latest.

Once they loaded up their gear and locked the house, the two men headed west for about ten miles at which time Mark signaled for Kevin to pull over. He wanted to double check one of the maps.

"Let's keep heading this way for another twenty, twenty-five. That should put us out in the boonies by mid-morning. We can still hit Decker's by eleven or so if we keep at a decent pace. The last time I was there, it was really amazing. What'cha think?"

Kevin nodded and gave an exaggerated salute. "You're the captain. I'm following you. Just don't get us lost like you did in the U.P., alright?"

"Shut up," Mark laughed. "You can lead on the way back if you're so friggin' worried about my navigational skills."

He shot Kevin 'the finger' and Kevin responded in kind. They laughed, flipped their kickstands up, and started out on the road toward Decker's Pond.

Mark and Kevin pedaled side by side along winding stretches of desolate roads, conversing part of the time and silently taking in the peaceful scenery that surrounded them during other times. Mark noticed a line of geese just up ahead that appeared to be guiding them. Kevin laughed, suggesting that GPS actually stood for geese pointing system. Later on, they both saw what they thought was either an eagle or a turkey vulture soaring overhead. Within minutes, it was joined by others, so Mark was convinced it had to be a vulture.

By 10:30am, hunger pangs had shifted from being a gentle mistress to an angry dominatrix who would not be ignored. Mark signaled to Kevin as he pulled up beside him. They slowed their pace as they pedaled next to each other.

"Yeah, it was stupid to skip breakfast. Let's eat now, I'm starving. How about over there? That looks like a decent spot," Mark said, pointing to a shady tree line.

"I like it. Let's do it, man."

They slowed even more until they were coasting through the tall grass toward the area. Mark dismounted first and ran alongside his bike for a few feet until coming to a complete stop. He put the kickstand down with his foot and watched as Kevin glided in. He squeezed the hand brakes and tried to pull his feet out of the toe clips but couldn't dislodge them in time.

"Shit! What the --" he shouted as he and his bike slammed into a large oak tree.

"What the hell, dude? Just learning to ride?" Mark said, jogging over to help his friend.

"I-I couldn't get my feet out of these damn toe clips in time. Here, give me a hand. They're still stuck."

Mark tried to move the bike out of the way as Kevin lifted his knees up toward his chest.

"Wait, wait! They're not coming out. I think my shoes are caught on something."

"Okay, hang on. Let me get a better look. Maybe your laces got tangled." Mark crawled down around the pedals. He untied Kevin's shoe laces, wrapped his hands around Kevin's right ankle and started to pry his foot away from the bike.

"Wait! Stop!" Kevin winced, looking down. "What are you *doing*, man?"

"Trying to get your foot out of the clip, what do you think? Let me try the other one. I'm going to shift the bike to the other side so I can get a clear shot at your shoe, okay?"

"Fine. Just hurry up. This is really fucked."

Mark pushed his friend, still attached to the bike, carefully onto his right side so he could pull his left leg out from confinement. Kevin strained his head and neck to see how the situation was progressing.

"Can you get *that* shoe out?"

"I'm trying," Mark grunted, jerking Kevin's leg backwards, away from the bike. "No, no, it's not coming out. I don't understand. Maybe try pulling your feet out again? You know, lift your heel out of your shoes first?"

"Alright, let me try." Kevin grunted and shifted his weight onto his elbows to get better leverage. As hard as he fought to free his feet from the shoes, he simply couldn't get any momentum.

"Fuck."

"Okay, let's not panic yet. I'm going to pour some water over your shoe. It's warm enough out here that it's possible your feet just swelled up. I mean, it's a shot, right?"

Mark uncapped one of the water bottles from his backpack and drained its contents over Kevin's shoe, sock, and left peddle.

"Try it now."

In a final attempt to free himself from the metal prison, Kevin yanked his leg up as hard and as fast as he could. A shock of pain seared up through his body.

"Fuck it! I can't! It's not working."

"Damn it. Didn't the water help *at all?*" Mark was frustrated for his friend, but partially *at* him as well.

Kevin raised his head slowly until his eyes met Mark's. He grimaced. A heavy blanket of pain encircled his foot. Beads of sweat trickled down both sides of his face. His body quivered with each breath. "I know this sounds like I'm shitting you, but I think my feet are...welded to the pedals."

"Are you fuckin' kidding me? Come on, you're just freaking out. I'll help you up and we'll ride over to Decker's where we can get a better handle on this. There's a bathroom there and probably some people that can help if we need it. Okay? Can you keep riding?"

"Yeah, yeah, I'll be alright. Just help me up, huh? This is only slightly awkward, if you know what I mean?" Kevin forced a laugh.

The last thing he wanted was for Mark to know exactly how scared he was. With a bit of effort and an enormous amount of coordination, Mark helped Kevin into an upright position before climbing onto his own bike. The two took off down the road, this time in complete silence.

The sun beat down, hard and angry. What was supposed to be a pleasant 70 degree day was edging closer to the 85 mark. Clouds or even a light rain would have been a welcome reprieve, but the day had its own agenda.

Sweat rolled down the backs of both bikers. By the time they hit Decker's Pond, they were coated in a sheen of glistening perspiration. Mark pedaled into the picnic area first and parked his bike. He waited for Kevin, who was about a minute behind him. Once Kevin was close enough, Mark helped guide his friend over to a red picnic bench. He grasped the front of the handlebars and steadied the bike so Kevin could lean against the top of the table for support.

"I've got it. Scoot back onto the table and I'll take a better look. I might have missed something when we stopped before."

Kevin steadied his hands and arms as he pushed himself up from the seat. He didn't budge.

"I can't."

"You can't what?"

"I can't get out of the seat, Mark. I'm stuck. Just like my feet."

"Bullshit. Quit screwing around and move back. I'm telling you, if this is your way of pissing around because I took the lead with the plans today..."

Kevin cut him off. He couldn't hide it any longer. "Mark, listen to me. *I can't*, alright? I'm not mad and I'm not fuckin' around. And if I could sit my ass on the table, I would. But *I can't*."

"Okay, Kev, calm down. Can you explain to me what you mean by 'I can't'?"

"You're going to think I'm nuts, but I'm dead serious. I-I'm attached to the seat. Adhered to it. I know that doesn't make sense, but you *know* me. Don't you think I would move from this damn thing if I could?"

Mark looked at his friend. Over the past fifteen years, they had their share of ups and downs. They fought over the same girls in high school, helped each other move into the dorms in college, and comforted each other after their buddy got killed in a car accident on his 21st birthday. But through it all, if there was one thing Mark could be certain of, it was Kevin's integrity.

"I know, man. Look, we've been sweating up a storm. Maybe, somehow, your body created some weird suction to the seat. Take my hand and I'll put you off."

"No. I think I just want to go home."

"Kevin. Come on..."

"Please, Mark. Don't make me beg you. I-I'm kinda freaked about this. I don't know what's going on and I sure as hell don't know *why* it's happening. But for some fuckin' reason, my body is attaching itself to the bike. *Look!*"

Kevin reached down and pulled his bike shorts up as far as he could. The skin from his inner thighs had *fused* with the seat. The only way he could tell where the leg ended and the bike's saddle began was by the difference in color between the two.

"Jesus," Mark whispered. He shot a look toward Kevin's feet. His shoes were hanging on by threads; most of the material had worn away or had been absorbed. Kevin's white athletic socks had disappeared completely. The pedals had become an assimilation of metal and flesh without any remnants of toe clips or reflectors. His feet were now two masses of alloy mixed with pulpy human tissue.

"What the *hell*?"

"I don't know!" Kevin screamed. "I just want to get out of here and get to a hospital!"

"Yeah, yeah, right. Of course. Can you ride?" he asked, cringing as the words left his mouth.

"It's the one thing I *can* do. Let's go, huh?" He forced a guttural chuckle.

Mark nodded and mounted his bike. He pedaled out in front to lead the way as Kevin followed. He glanced behind him, making sure that his friend was actually able to keep up. He figured they had at least a two hour ride ahead of them, and that would be without stopping to eat or piss or deal with any other weird shit. Mark's mind raced through different scenarios, trying to come up with some kind of reason for this anomaly.

After a few minutes, he hit his brakes hard, skidded to a dusty stop and turned around to face Kevin who was about a hundred meters behind.

"Hey, I just thought of something. Remember the guy at the bike shop? How he was trying to talk us out of buying them? Maybe *he* knows something."

Mark froze. As his friend got closer, he could see that Kevin's hands and forearms had become integrated into the frame of the bike.

"Go! Don't stop, Mark. Keep going!"

He shuddered; he covered his mouth with his hands. Mark was caught between wanting to scream and needing to cry. Without a word, he turned around and started pedaling, this time much faster. He heard gears clicking behind him. He tried and failed to stifle sobbing gasps as he imagined Kevin's own knuckle joints as the gear shifts.

Don't look behind you. Don't turn around. Ride straight to the emergency entrance at the hospital, stay long enough to get him some help, and then get the hell out of there until they fix him.

As they road, Mark thought they might be able to take a short cut by the Beeson Farm. If nothing else, that could save them at least fifteen minutes. If Kevin could push a *little* more, just pedal a *little* faster...

God. He thought about Kevin's feet and the monstrosity of what they had become. He wanted to vomit, but instead turned his head to the side and shouted as loud as he could about his shortcut idea.

"Did you hear me, Kev?"

Mark slowed down and steered to his left, looping around in a semi-circle to ride alongside his friend. He yanked his hands off the handlebars and covered his mouth to suffocate a scream.

Kevin's torso was now fused with the crossbar. His arms and legs were no longer distinguishable from the metal and rubber of the machine. A very misshapen head sat in place of the headlight that was set in between the handlebars. Orange reflectors blinked on and off where eyes had once been. A tiny mound of flesh and nostril hair had formed into the shape of a horn.

"Holy shit!" Mark shrieked into his cupped hands. "I'll get help. I'll...get...help..." he sputtered. Mark tried to adjust his position on his bike, to lean forward in order to gain some speed, but his shoes refused to come out of the toe clips.

He pedaled away in a chaotic fury, but didn't dare look down at his feet.

IMPOSSIBLE

M rs. Lawrence Covington and her annual charity dinners had been shrouded in secrecy for the past forty years. Known in her earlier life as Abigail Bagby, she married into the Covington fortune after graduating from Randall University, class of 1927, with a degree in journalism. However, instead of venturing into the working world, she and Lawrence Covington wed. He promptly whisked her away, inducting her into a wealthy and extravagant lifestyle where she never had the opportunity to put her degree to good use.

In 1977, after Lawrence passed away from an unfortunate encounter with a plate of bad oysters, Abigail was left as the sole heiress to the great Covington Corporation. The seventy-three year old woman became a recluse, only venturing out from her enormous estate when the need was imperative to do so. After 1978, no one ever saw Mrs. Covington without a black veil over her face, and that included her servants and personal attendants. It was assumed she wore the cover out of a sense of mourning and respect for her departed husband.

Since its inception in 1915, the Covington Corporation hosted an annual charity dinner, with all the proceeds going to the local homeless lodges and shelters. It was seen as a valiant effort to keep older orphaned children and vagrants out of the jails and poorhouses. Over the years, Lawrence and Abigail began restricting the press from attending the event. It had become something of a circus; a popularity show with photographers snapping candids of the local celebrities and papers running outlandish 'who's who' headlines in order to compete with one another. By the early 60s, the press was deemed persona non grata – no one working for newspapers, television, or radio was allowed entrance.

Which is why I, newbie journalist, Rachel Walsh, was stunned when I walked into work this morning. My editor, Paul Grange, handed me an envelope and told me I had just landed an exclusive assignment. Paul is one of those Lou Grant wannabees; the tough exterior with the heart of gold, just not as famous or as talented.

Our paper, The Lakeland Reader, is about two levels up from a tabloid gossip rag, but it still provides me with an honest living and allows me to put a rented room over my head and halfway-decent food on the table. The paper enjoys a fairly large readership, but we're not exactly the best game in town. If I were a betting gal, I'd put my money on our humor columnist and the crossword puzzle as the main reason our sales aren't circling the drain.

We've just never been the hard-hitting news source that a city our size requires. Instead, we end up leaving the *real* news to the big guys while we focus on stories like the snake that got away and somehow ended up in the toilet at the Lexington Street Derry's Bakery, licking Mr. Edwards' right buttock.

After Paul presented me with the big manila envelope, I opened it and stood there like an idiot, complete with mouth hanging open and eyes as wide as the proverbial saucer.

"I thought we were banned from these charity dinners years ago," I finally blurted out.

"We were. But I guess we're back in. Maybe old lady Covington has seen the light and wants some press after all. Anyway, I'm giving the gig to you, Rachel. Run with it and don't look back."

I nodded and told him I'd be honored.

Throughout the week leading up to the dinner, my co-workers took turns either congratulating me or giving me their condolences. The word on the street was that The Lakeland Reader was the only member of the press that was invited, and in turn, I would represent the whole of print media. I wasn't sure if that was something to be proud of or embarrassed by, but I had a job to do and I liked getting a paycheck. I was committed.

I spent time researching the Covington Corporation, Lawrence and Abigail, and the rest of the family, but I didn't come up with any particularly juicy leads or clues that sent up red flags. Most of the information revolved around the business and the charity work – certainly nothing to write home about.

My only issue was that shortly after Mr. Covington died, Mrs. Covington went into hiding. I couldn't find an article, interview, or even a simple press release dated past 1969, with the exception of Lawrence's obituary in '77. I started to wonder if they really did have something to hide or did they just hate the media that much?

The Lakeland Hotel, built in 1927, was the pinnacle of the entire city block. The art deco design gave it a flavor of science-fiction coupled with a dab of otherworldliness. This was in comparison to the smaller, dirty grey rectangular buildings which surrounded it. It was beautiful, a real landmark. I could see why anyone would want to host a special function in a place like that. It couldn't help but command attention with the stylized geometric patterns running from the ground all the way to the top floor.

Two doormen clad in red, tight-at-the-waist jackets and black pleated pants stood guard at the entryway which led to the lobby.

Without a word, the man on the right gripped the smooth lacquered handle of the door and allowed me to enter.

The place was abuzz with activity; B-list celebrities, wealthy businessmen with their dolled up wives, the board of directors for some of the more prominent companies in the city – all of them rubbing elbows and comparing wallet sizes for lack of something else to do while they waited for the meal to be served and the festivities to begin.

I had arrived just past 6pm, toting a tiny recorder and paper (just in case) for the interview. It was a lesson I learned the hard way – always bring paper and something to write with, for only those in heaven know if a mechanical device such as a recorder is involved, it will surely break down at the last minute.

I hoped to make a good impression. I wasn't only representing The Lakeland Reader, but all of print media. It had been so long since any reporter was welcome here; I wanted to come across as competent and prepared, and to be honest, get on Mrs. Covington's good side. I was going to win her over. That was my plan. Like any young, aspiring writer, I was already imagining how I would deal with my new found fame. Television appearances, my face on the cover of magazines, even radio spots. I would be legendary -- all due to my superior skills as the first reporter to break the Covington story after decades of silence.

The beautiful atmosphere of Avery Hall, the room where the dinner was taking place, was a visual nirvana. Everything from the curtains to the floor was stunning. Tables were decked out with colorful candles reflecting back on mirrored pedestals. Flower petals were strewn over satin table cloths. It was like stepping back in time where elegance, down to the finest detail, was not overlooked.

But there was something else...something *peculiar.*

It was off-putting, to say the least. There was a distinct odor, a high note above all the festivities that struck me in the most disturbing way. The smell reminded me of a combination between roses, perfume, and formaldehyde. The scented candles on each of the tables were doing their best to cover the foulness of the stench, but unfortunately were losing the battle.

People mingled around the edges of the room, talking quietly among themselves. By my count, there were at least a hundred guests, maybe more. This was certainly an affluent crowd; each one dressed better than the next. I considered myself rather lucky to be in the presence of high society for an assignment such as this one. However, as I made my way through the room, I detected a strong sense of indignation. Some of the guests were not pleased by my presence. Out of the corner of my eye, I saw heads turning in my direction and heard angry murmurs.

"Tough crowd," I whispered to myself in order to quell my own anxiety. I made a mental note to remind Paul that he was going to owe me lunch for having to deal with such elite snobs for a whole evening.

A hostess approached just in time to save me from more aimless wandering among the throngs of distain.

"You must be the reporter Mrs. Covington was expecting. She had us set a table for you. Would you follow me?"

"Of course, thank you. Um, miss?"

"Yes, ma'am?"

"Do you have any information about this dinner? For example, can you tell me who these other guests are or how they got invited? Also, have you met Mrs. Covington personally?"

She didn't answer. She just smiled at me and held out a chair at a table set for one.

While the final speaker finished her fundraising pitch and the dishes were being cleared away, a young man came out from backstage. He set up a dark, wooden podium in the center of the raised platform and adjusted the microphone by tilting it downward.

A jittery hush washed over the room as the lights were dimmed, providing a sultry shade of twilight. A shrouded figure shuffled to the lectern; one hand gripping a cane to aide a stilted gait. With a gloved, claw-like hand, the living silhouette reached out to touch the mic. An ear splitting shriek of feedback swept the room. I couldn't help but cringe at the sound, but noticed that every other eye was riveted to the person on the stage. They were completely unaffected by the noise.

The veiled shadow leaned forward and spoke.

I wasn't sure what to expect, having never heard Mrs. Covington's voice. I suppose I assumed she would sound like a grandmother, or maybe a salty old woman who locks herself away for years at a time. Instead, the lilting voice of a young woman filled the room. She thanked everyone for attending and reassured them that their charitable gifts would benefit the homeless.

The disconnect between what I knew of the shrouded figure and what I was hearing was jarring to say the least. According to my research, Mrs. Covington would be well into her eighties by now. No octogenarian would sound like that. I supposed it was possible that she was one of those incredulous people who never aged and was as spry as a spring hen, but more than likely, there was some other explanation.

As she concluded her speech, the hostess escorted me to the backstage area. I took a seat at a small metal table, placed the recorder in front of the seat across from me and waited. It wasn't long before the burgundy curtain rustled and a black gloved hand found its edge.

"Mrs. Covington," I said, extending my hand. "It's a real pleasure and honor to meet you. I can't tell you how much I appreciate you allowing our paper to do an exclusive interview."

She didn't return my greeting or acknowledge my outstretched hand. Instead, she sat in the chair across from me and pushed the recorder aside. I watched. I waited. I wasn't sure if I should just start asking questions. Before I could open my mouth, she lifted her veil. What happened after that is somewhat of a blur.

Her *head*.

Her *face.*

I couldn't comprehend what I was seeing. Her head was a skull, *a grinning corpse's head.* Shards of tissue hung precariously from her cheekbones and jaw. Wispy strands of white stringy hair hung limp where her ears had been. Her mouth was simply a ghastly row of clenched teeth held together by nothing more than sheer will. But her eyes…God, that was the worst. Eye sockets dark and wide, yet each one contained a perfectly round eyeball tethered to what had to be a vein or tendon or some such anatomical horror.

Could this thing see me? Is this a fucking prank? A joke at the reporter's expense? I was shaken from my frozen terror by a grotesque clicking sound. *Oh my God! It's trying to talk!*

The jaw opened and closed as if trying to speak, but there were no lips or tongue to formulate words. I could, however, hear a guttural croak coming from deep within its death head. It told me to ask my questions.

My eyes darted around the curtained area, desperately looking for a way out. I realized that I was hyperventilating. I felt my heart pounding inside my chest. Without even touching my face, I knew I had broken out in a cold sweat. My mouth was dry. If it weren't attached, I probably would have swallowed my own tongue. I was shaking so badly, I lost the grip on my pen.

"I think you dropped this," the corpse of Mrs. Covington hissed.

As she bent over to pick it up, her forearm exposed itself from the long, black sleeve. What I saw between her black glove and the end of her jacket was inconceivable -- mottled grey skin barely covering exposed tendons and bone. There were no muscles to speak of. My brain was screaming.

How can this monstrosity function?

"Thank you," I choked and took the pen, trying not to touch this hideous nightmare.

Mrs. Covington's jaw opened slightly, creaked once, then snapped shut with a hideous pop. She turned her head to face me. I wanted to vomit, but I couldn't even commit to that. I was mesmerized by unearthly fear.

"Your questions!" It hissed again.

I tried to formulate words, but I couldn't find my voice. I stammered. I made a few non-descript utterances. I took deep breaths that only made me more lightheaded than I already was.

Mrs. Covington stood up and moved closer to me. Before I could blink, her black gloved claw hooked onto my shoulder and dug deep into my sweater. I felt the bony points of her fingers embedding themselves into my skin. Her body was so close to mine that every time I inhaled, I took in a putrid mix of formaldehyde and decomposing rot. I made a feeble effort to turn my head but felt faint.

"You reporters are all alike. You disgust me with your quests for fame and publicity," the raspy voice groaned from the skull's gaping maw. "It was different in my day. We knew good journalism from the yellow trash you put out now."

Her face was now inches from mine. I stared into the lifeless sockets that somehow held its eyes in their black abyss. I wanted to cry, to run, to move, but I couldn't. All I could manage to do was to stare eye to hideous eye with this ghastly version of hell.

"You didn't look too closely at the other guests I take it," she said.

I shook my head and she continued.

"Not all of them were donors. Some had been reporters. Just like you."

"I don't understand," I managed to squeak.

"You will," she wheezed and released me. She reached her skeletal arm up to her head and lowered the veil. With another click of her jaw, Mrs. Covington turned on her heels with the help of her cane and shuffled through the part in the curtain.

Seconds later, I passed out.

I don't recall what happened after that. All I remember is waking up in my apartment the next morning. At first, I wasn't even sure that the interview actually took place. Nerves can do crazy things to a person's psyche, including inducing over-the-top nightmares. I initially chalked it up to having had a few drinks – I would check my notes tomorrow.

My immediate plan was to hit the shower and take a leisurely stroll to the corner café. After a horrid dream like that, this Sunday was going to be all about me. I was hereby distancing myself from all work-related tasks for the next 24 hours.

As I threw off the blanket, a partially opened envelope fell to the floor next to my bed. I looked and saw that it was an invitation to a charity event for the following year. I reached down to pick it up and caught a quick glimpse of my forearm. My flesh was decomposing before my eyes, falling away to the carpet like old, brittle strips of newspaper. I lifted my head and stared into the mirror which hung on the opposite wall.

Oh, my God.

My head...

My face...

SPOONS

The idea had already been floating around in my brain by the
time I heard my alarm go off. I stayed in bed and pretended to
be asleep, listening as he gathered up his things and left for work. I
waited until I heard the truck pull away before getting out of bed. I
didn't want any confrontations today or any day. I didn't even want to
look at him again -- not with what I had planned to do. Once I knew
he was truly off the premises, I breathed a sigh of relief. I was alone.

Well, I wasn't *actually* alone, per se. My two cats kept me company. It was just that the thought of him being out of the house and
physically away from me was comforting. I stood in the hallway, debating if I should call in to work and tell them I wasn't feeling well
or just go in and suck it up for another endless day.

The thought of taking a shower, getting dressed, and driving
to my job made me exhausted. I could picture myself sitting at my
desk, ghosting through my job, forcing small talk in the elevator,
moving blindly through the entire day as if I weren't connected to
my own body. Having to sludge through eight hours, only to come
home to the hell that waited for me was too overwhelming.

It was 7:45am. I was supposed to be at work by 8:30am. Even if I
skipped the shower and threw my clothes on from yesterday, I would
barely make it. I decided to call in sick. I still hadn't made any defin-
itive plans at that point, but I didn't have the energy to rush through
a morning routine and then arrive late to work on top of it.

I went into the bathroom. The stark whiteness of the walls matched my pale, sullen complexion. I stared into the mirror and hated what I saw. It wasn't a critical commentary about my physical appearance, but rather a reflection of despair. The misery and emptiness were unyielding. My 32-year-old face looked aged and worn.

I toyed with the idea of taking a shower for no other reason than to clear my head, but it felt like too much effort. Instead, I hoisted myself up on the bathroom counter next to the sink and rested my head against my knees. I had made it this far in the day, almost a whole hour of wakefulness without crying, but the tearless moments were slipping away. Sobs welled up from my gut as I blinked back tears, not wanting them to come. I knew that if I started to cry, there would be no reason to stop. Finally, they came, streaming down my face, warm against my skin.

I couldn't hold it in any longer. At the same time, one of the cats jumped up and rubbed against my leg. I reached out to pet her, thankful for the connection. I wondered who would take care of the cats. *He* certainly wouldn't. If he barely took notice of *me*, his wife, there would be no way in hell he'd spend a moment out of his day caring for my *cats*.

I picked up the bottle of antidepressants that was next to me on the counter. I had just renewed the prescription a couple of days before, so the bottle was almost full.

It would be so easy; one pill at a time until they were gone. I thought about writing a note, but how on earth would I explain the past ten years? A note like that could go on forever. It would be a pretty weak summary of how horrible and worthless he made me feel every single day. While it was true that he never *hit* me, his choice of words, his constant condescension, and the public criticisms had worn me down over time.

During the first few years, I foolishly believed the confrontations and disagreements between us were just a matter of two different personalities trying to iron out relationship wrinkles. But he was a quick study in the art of degradation, and what little self-esteem I had at the beginning of our time together had completely vanished by the third year. *If I were stronger, if I spoke up more, if I knew how to stand up for myself* -- all of these ifs never made a bit of difference. I was who I was and didn't know any better at the time.

I shook the plastic pill bottle and opened the lid. More tears flowed and I set the bottle back down. I buried my head against my knees again; my brain reeled back and forth. In one moment, I almost felt a thread of strength and dignity, but in the very next, I couldn't imagine living one more hour under these circumstances.

The most recent wrench thrown into this nightmare of a relationship was the possibility of being pregnant with this man's child. It was the most revolting conundrum I had ever faced. I was a week late already and had what I believed were early symptoms. We never talked about having kids. We never talked about much of anything. We didn't even have sex all that often. It was like one of those unspoken rules - if it was Friday night and he wasn't busy doing something else, the marital obligation (expectation) was probably going to be fulfilled.

I went downstairs to the kitchen to get a large glass of water. I never could swallow pills dry. As I stood at the sink, my eyes drifted to a white plastic serving spoon in a ceramic jar which sat next to the stove. My stomach cramped as I plucked it out of the container and held it. There was nothing unique about it. It was a simple, long handled spoon, one that could be found in a department store's kitchen section for about a buck and a half. I gripped the handle in one hand and the bowl in the other and snapped it in two. Shards of plastic flew against the kitchen window. A large piece scuttled across the vinyl floor and came to rest near a broom that leaned in the corner.

He had given me that spoon for my last birthday. The year before that, my gift was the red plastic serving spoon which sat in the same jar next to the oven. Every birthday, since the time he and I began dating over a decade ago, was marked with a similar spoon as a present. He would hand me a crinkled brown paper bag, without a card accompanying it, and say 'happy birthday'. The routine was always the same. After giving it to me, he would stand there, waiting for me to thank him for being so considerate.

When we were first dating, I thought this spoon ceremony was kind of funny, sort of a private joke between the two of us. But then it went on for a second year, then a third, and then it wasn't funny anymore. It was sad and pathetic and heartbreaking. When I asked him if this was really my birthday present, my *real* present and not just a gag gift, he looked me square in the eye and said 'of course it was.' Apparently, it was my fault for having made an offhand comment about needing to buy some spoons for my apartment when we had first met.

He was clearing $50,000 and that was during the first half of the marriage. He never let me see his pay stubs after his company gave him his first raise, but I was certain that money was never a problem for him. I wasn't looking for an extravagant present. I never thought of myself as an extravagant person. But I had hoped, year after year, for something more than a plastic spoon from a discount store.

I wandered into the bedroom. I hadn't fully committed to my idea yet, so I was aimlessly drifting from one room to the next. I stared at the bed, *our* bed, which was set dead center in the middle of the room between the two windows. The blankets were bunched up in a crumpled ball and one of the cats was perched on top of the lump of material. I forced a smile.

Being intimate with *me* was never a priority for him, but he was certainly quick to notice beautiful women when we were out. The times we *were* intimate felt forced and smacked of obligation. On the third night, after we were married, a creepy little spider was crawling up the wall on my side of the bed. I have always been afraid of them, so I asked my new husband, who was next to me in bed reading, if he would kill it. His response was to slam his book shut and throw it across the room.

"Why can't you do anything yourself?" he yelled right before he took *my* pillow and threw it at the spider. I watched in horror and disgust as both arachnid and pillow slid down the wall to the floor. *Three days,* I thought.

It was in that precise moment when I realized that my life had spun out of control; that I was just beginning the downward spiral into depression and despair. The crumb of self-esteem I had was crushed under the weight of his pointed and vile accusation. This is what my life had become.

I walked into the smallest room of the house; the den, or *'my computer room,'* as he referred to it. He spent most of his time in front of the machine. This included lunch, dinner, and a large portion of most weekends. My own desk had been crowded into a corner, tucked away from his sprawl.

I paid the household bills sitting at that desk. From my annual salary of $16,000, a real pittance compared to his, I put in my half toward all the bills. This often left me with no money until the next paycheck. I had holes in my jeans and pairs of shoes that were worn through, yet he never offered as much as a single dime to help me replace anything.

He, however, had plenty of money to afford week-long trips for himself, which he took three or four times a year. He and his friends would charter boats, hike in the mountains, or go on scuba diving vacations. I don't know for a fact if the other wives went along, but from some of the pictures I saw, there looked to be a fair representation of women in attendance.

For a moment, I sat at my desk and looked at the pile of bills. I started crying again, burdened with the thought of divorce and how that was not a viable option for me, especially if I was pregnant. I knew myself well enough to know that I couldn't raise a child on my own, financially or otherwise.

I felt sick, trapped, broke, and desperate. I got up from my desk, went back into the bathroom and opened the bottle of pills. I lined up each yellow tablet next to one another and silently counted them. *Fifty-four.* Three days shy of a full bottle. I looked up and saw my reflection in the large bathroom mirror. Hair unkempt, face reddened and wet, I couldn't help but believe with everything in my being that this was the only way out of my living hell.

I pulled down a paper cup from the holder that was attached to the wall. I filled it with cold water and swallowed it quickly. I remembered having read about this particular drug's overdose reactions and knew what to expect.

Everything would slow down; my heart rate, my breathing, and my ability to think. Next, shaking and chills would set in. The capacity to warm up, regardless of how many blankets were piled on would be gone. I might throw up. Eventually, I would just fade off to sleep. In a very broad sense, all of that sounded more peaceful than being kicked and shoved over to the edge of the bed every night because I might accidentally touch him while we slept. It also sounded better than being verbally attacked because I bought a three dollar garbage can for the kitchen without consulting him first.

I filled the cup again and stared at the line of medication in front of me. As I reached for the first pill, I felt a drip run down my inner thigh. My period had just begun.

An ambulance and a town fire truck sped down the street and stopped in front of the house. Flashing lights and loud sirens coaxed neighbors to investigate from the safety of their porches and front windows. Three EMTs and one fireman hustled to the door wheeling a black cot and carrying large bags of medical supplies. They knocked and rang the doorbell simultaneously. I stumbled to the door in order to open it, but one of the EMTs was already pushing his way in.

"Are you the one who called for an ambulance?"

I nodded.

"Are you the individual needing assistance?"

I started crying and mumbled incoherently. I felt lightheaded and swooned backwards. The fireman caught me before I collapsed to the floor. He led me over to the couch and sat down next to me. The others gathered around.

"Can you tell us what the problem is?"

"Upstairs..."

"What? What's upstairs?"

"He...he just..." I choked out.

"*He?* There's someone else in the home?" the man asked. He grabbed for his two-way radio and glanced up the stairs.

"My husband. He...he just...fainted. I didn't know what to do."

The three EMTs bolted up the stairs and left me on the couch. The fireman opened the front door and went outside to clear the way. I could hear snippets of conversations, bags opening, procedures being tried. Minutes later, I watched as they carried him down the stairs on the gurney, an oxygen mask over his face. One of the EMTs came over to me.

"We're taking him to St. Thomas. You can follow us in your car or ride in the ambulance, but we're leaving this minute."

"Thank you. I'll get my things and meet you at the hospital."

He nodded and left to join the others in the ambulance. I went to close the door and noticed all the neighbors still standing around slack-jawed, straining their necks to get a glimpse of some good old-fashioned tragedy for their evening's entertainment.

I went into the kitchen, turned on the hot water, and picked up the sponge. The blender had been soaking all day. I washed it and set it in the dish rack to air dry. Then, I took his empty glass from the sink, the one that held the milkshake I made for him hours ago, and cleaned it out as well.

ABOUT THE AUTHOR

Sue Rovens is an indie suspense and horror writer who lives in Normal, Illinois. She has written two novels, *Badfish* and *Track 9*, and a collection of creepy, short stories, *In A Corner, Darkly, Volume 1*. This is her second anthology. All are available on Amazon in paperback and Kindle formats.

She has appeared at Printers Row Lit Fest in Chicago numerous times, as well as Chambana-Con in Normal, Illinois, Duncan Manor Blue Fest in Towanda, Illinois, Books 2 Benefit, and at the Princeton Library Author Fair in Princeton, Illinois. Sue is a current member of the Chicago Writers Association.

For more information on Sue, her books, and her upcoming appearances, please visit suerovens.com.

If you enjoyed this book, please consider posting a review on amazon.com or any other social media page. Thanks!